3 1111 01389 2631

LIVERPOOL JMU LIBRARY

WITHDRAWN

LIVERPOOL JOHN MOORES UNIVERSITY
Aldham Robarts L.R.C.
TEL. 0151 231 3701/3834

D15136578

First published in Great Britain in 2008 by Comma Press
www.commapress.co.uk

'The Award' was first published as *Son Tramvay* ('The Last Tram') in 1991.
'Midnight on the Outside' previously appeared in *Muntasaf Layl al-Ghurba* (Maktabat al-Usra, Cairo 1997) . 'Amman's Birds Sweep Low' first appeared in *Tuyour Amman Tuhalliq Munkhafida* (1981). A shorter version of 'There's No Room for a Lover in this City' appeared in *My Brother Is Looking for Rimbaud* (Arabic Cultural Center, Beirut/Dar Al-Baida 2005). 'Meningtis' first appeared in *Vered* (Tel AvivHaklbbutz-Hame'ukhd, 2006).

Lines taken from THE MEANING OF RELATIVITY by Albert Einstein first published by Vieweg, 1922, and by Princeton University Press in 1996. Reprinted by permission of Princeton University Press.

Copyright © for all stories remains with the authors
Copyright © for all translations remains with the translators
Copyright © for this selection belongs to Comma Press
All rights reserved.

The right of the authors and translators to be identified as such has been asserted in accordance with the Copyright Designs and Patent Act 1988

The moral right of the authors and translators has been asserted.

This collection is entirely a work of fiction. The names, characters and incidents portrayed in it are the work of the author's imagination. Any resemblance to actual persons, living or dead, events or localities, is entirely coincidental. The publisher does not always share the opinions of the authors.

A CIP catalogue record of this book is available from the British Library

ISBN: 1905583206
EAN: 978-1905583201

The publishers gratefully acknowledge assistance from the Arts Council England North West, and also the support of Literature Northwest.

literaturenorthwest ●

Set in Bembo by David Eckersall
Printed and bound in England by SRP Ltd, Exeter.

MADINAH

City Stories from the Middle East

Edited by
JOUMANA HADDAD

To L.

CONTENTS

CONTENTS

Introduction

Cities and literature have always been intertwined. Joyce's Dublin, Auster's New York, Mahfouz's Cairo and Pamuk's Istanbul are just four instances – among countless – where the global/extraverted consciousness of a place has converged with the private/withdrawn consciousness of an author, or, to be more accurate, with the way an author personally experiences, lives, outlives and is, in turn, outlived by his or her urban space.

Yes, cities are doomed to be entangled with the writing they've inspired. Even the invisible, unnamed, avoided and despised cities (precisely *because* they are invisible, unnamed, avoided and despised). After all, isn't a 'negative', passive reality often stronger than a direct and tangible one? Isn't the undisclosed more haunting and omnipresent than the openly confessed and easily mentioned? I firmly believe it is.

Indeed, cities and literature are knotted together. There is so much evidence to support this. Call it osmosis or the free communication of ideas, but the relationship between them can be, at times, damaging and cruel (I'm thinking of Kafka's Prague, so charged with an underground hidden sensibility for horror, drama and self-destruction), at others cathartic, political, equipped to expose social diseases like corruption and inequality (take Balzac's Paris), but also stirring and even 'light' sometimes (Moravia's weightless Rome). But an elucidation seems at this point necessary: when I say 'city', I do not solely mean the place. I do not just mean the streets, the buildings, the traffic lights, the gradients, the markets, and the other details and textures that compose, and sometimes decompose, a tangible, physical geography. For a city is clearly much more complex than its concrete existence. It is the layout of a history, the architecture of a soul, the poetic of a vocation. A sum of sounds, smells, stories, dreams, plans, lies, fears, moments of suffering and bliss, and, I reluctantly add, of memories. A momentum of all the love stories it has witnessed, for instance, and of all the potential, latent ones that it is bound to witness tomorrow. Of all its births, deaths and re-births. A city is, in a word, its *destiny*. Its past, present, and most importantly, its future.

★

'Good writing makes life worth living,' says Harold Pinter. Undeniably, when we reach into the rich variety of novels, stories, poems and plays which constitute the wide sphere of Middle Eastern literatures (the plural is meant to express my scepticism towards such, and any other categorisation), we read works that say something worth saying, and say it, most importantly, with a talent and an artistry that are superior enough, and resilient enough, to survive through times and languages.

But unfortunately, the translation of this region's literatures, and particularly of Arabic literary works, into English, is not as dynamic as it should be. A key reason for this shortage might be that there are 22 different Arab countries and yet, these are consistently viewed as a whole – a whole referred to as the 'Arab World'. People tend to speak of 'Arabic Literature' rather than Lebanese Literature, Jordanian Literature, Syrian Literature and so on… Another reason is that very often, though not in all cases, Western publishers only choose to translate notorious names or works that have been censored in their own country (indeed, censorship has almost become a guarantee of translation, celebrity and financial prosperity), or works from areas which are in a state of crisis. What about the other equally talented, yet less famous writers? What about the excellent, yet uncensored, 'non sensationalist' works? What about the books that don't have titles like 'The Veiled Mistress' or 'Passion Under The Tent'?

The scarcity of first-rate Arabic literature available in English (and to a certain extent, vice-versa) is extremely unfortunate. It deprives both worlds of a better understanding of each other at a time when mutual comprehension has become vital. A greater flow of translation would allow both worlds to discover and cherish each others' cultural treasures and true essence, rather than focusing on prejudices, clichés, distorted views, narrow=minded judgments and false, media fabricated symbols.

Which brings us inevitably to the importance of literary endeavours such as this book. A project which puts together ten different cities, ten different cultures, ten different personal and public figures, and three different languages: Arabic, Turkish and Hebrew.

★

At this point, allow me to confess the following: it hasn't been at all easy for me, as the humble editor of this book, to choose just ten writers and ten stories from the broad realm of works that were available to me, and that are significant enough to deserve translation into English.

But an anthology is an anthology, and I *had* to choose. While doing so, I tried to combine my desire to introduce new talented voices, with the importance of including firmly established writers, side by side. I also favoured cities that are not much talked about – like Dubai, Latakia, Alexandria and Akka – alongside others that have forever enjoyed a high profile and a somehow mythical 'reputation' in literature – like

Baghdad, Beirut or Istanbul. Six of the stories here have been written, or rewritten especially for this project, the other four being taken from earlier collections published in their native countries. Together they take us on a hypothetical tour of the region, starting with Nedim Gürsel's tender story of one man's return, after decades of exile, and ending with Hassan Blasim's story of a refugee fleeing the chaos of Baghdad, thus turning the book full circle.

Vis-à-vis the Arabic stories, I evidently had a preference for those where the poetics of the language do not dominate the fictional dimension of the prose. Indeed, Arabic language takes a certain pride in the richness of its analogies, its symbols and synonyms. Why, for example, run the risks of saying 'breast' when you can wax lyrical about hills or mountains? Why hurt the 'sensitivity' of the reader by mentioning the clitoris, when you can use the mind's eye to describe it as the 'flower of paradise' or the 'lip of heaven', or – if you are really talented – the 'volcano's doorknob'? Such writing I have tried to avoid, mainly because I was striving to represent a new kind of fiction being produced in the region, one that uses, among many other characteristics, modern tools, and is more unswerving, bold and straight to the point.

The result is, hopefully, a colorful, diversified yet strangely consistent, convincing and harmonious puzzle. A puzzle which could be read, with a bit of willpower and a good amount of imagination, like the compilation of ten different chapters telling the same story over and over again: a story of alienation, exile (whether real or metaphoric), and solitude. Three themes which remind us Middle-Easterners (and my cynicism here is definitely not a luxury) why cities had to be invented in the first place.

As you take your trip through this book, you will notice that one of its main axes is the process of estrangement, whether by the time or – in Nedim Gürsel and Gamal al-Ghitani's cases – by the place. Another frequent feature is the fluidity of the urban space. As you read you will sense the topology of the city changing rapidly: one minute the street is a setting for a conversation, a moment of private, quiet contemplation, the next it's alive with a public demonstration, or some momentous, shared event, where the character is unable to be anything but swept along. You will witness tempos crossing; modulations in speed, in time with these significant transformations of physical space.

None of the stories in this book pretends (or *in*tends) to be 'representative' of the city, or country, they're based in. They rather use the city the way an artist might use a canvas. And all but one take place in the cities they're dedicated, the exception being Alexandria in Gamal al-Ghitani's story, 'Midnight on the Outside'. Here the city is merely longed for; a longing expressed through the desperate and impossible love between Youssef and Samia, and the labyrinthine process by which a character may be torn apart. It is worth mentioning that this story is the oldest on the list, and was written in 1969, set amid the mass depression that hit the Arab world after the defeat of 1967.

Fadwa al-Qasem, in 'The Week Before the Wife Arrived', set in Dubai, tackles in a subtle and intelligent way the theme of adultery. The author uses a reverse chronological structure to bring new emphasis and meaning to the minor details and daily rituals that, ultimately, make up a life. Here, despite expectation, and beneath the seducing temptation of lies, we discover a soul in pain, articulated by a certain slowness or clinical iciness, in the overall action.

Ala Hlehel's story, 'The Passport', set in the Palestinian town of Akka during the 2006 Israeli war on Lebanon, is a strong, ironic representation of what I would call 'the misunderstanding' in absolute. It should also be understood whilst rendered here in the single language of English, it describes a people living in two languages: Arabic and Hebrew. The opening phone conversation, for instance, and the later insults hurled by a carload of Israeli youths, would have been in Hebrew. In the original Hlehel distinguished these passages for his audience, by writing them in *al-Fus-ha*, classical Arabic, but in the story the Palestinians, like in everyday life, would be expected to understand.

Yitzhak Laor, in 'Meningitis', set in Tel Aviv, takes the perspective of Yair, a sympathetic, if naïve, soldier, in order to criticise and lampoon the Israeli military perspective. He expresses, throughout the daily life of Yair, portrayed with a talent for the nuances and the unsaid, a courageous position against the hypocrisies of the Israeli government's thinking, which falls in line with all of Laor's wider career as a writer and intellectual.

Youssef Al Mohaimeed's story, 'There's No Room for a Lover in this City', set in Riyadh, explores the many contradictions of a city that suffers from the same asphyxiation it inflicts on its own people. Yet a strong wind of change is almost palpable throughout the paragraphs, while the main character struggles to live out what his geography denies him. There is also a high praise of the imagination, one of the best utensils in a human being's survival kit.

Nedim Gürsel, in 'The Award', set in Istanbul, takes the components of his city, one by one dismantles them then reconstructs them as he fancies. There is a cry of ownership, of territoriality, yet in a very poetic and tender way. A longing for what is lying there and waiting to be taken. It is a story of solitude and recent history, but mainly of defeat, a story where the city and the woman become one, only to make the feeling of loss even crueler.

Elias Farkouh's story, 'Amman's Birds Sweep Low', set in Amman, invests its five characters with a variety of personalities that convey the atmosphere and the characteristics of the city itself. Here the human being is just another aspect of the place. The faces' features and the streets, the bodies and the buildings become indistinguishable. Inside a car, jammed between Nisreen, Khalaf, Titi, Ibrahim and the car owner, we do not discover Amman. We dig into it.

Hasan Blasim's 'The Reality and the Record', set in

Baghdad, immerses us in mayhem. There is a powerful feeling that the protagonist was born in the wrong country in the wrong time; a great sense of cosmic bad luck, which although it makes him feel alone is, ironically, a common, binding feeling across many of the characters in this story, and indeed throughout the anthology. There is also a sense of urgency, a rush towards a point that cannot be seen nor foreseen, which heightens the reigning chaos and confusion.

Absurdity and helplessness are also key notes in Nabil Sulayman's 'City of Crimson', set in Latakia. Here we meet Wasif, a tired, sedated, almost life-exhausted character, deployed by the author in order to reflect a sleeping, frozen, anaesthetised city. There is a slow-motion rhythm in the narrative which makes the bloody, final crescendo even more shocking, like a slap in the face – possibly in the face of a city which needs to be awoken from its numbness.

In 'Living it Up (and Down) in Beirut', I opted to stand further towards the experimental end of the book's spectrum. In a back and forth movement between the main body of the text (written in the central character's voice) and the third person footnotes, between time present and time past and four key dates in Beirut's history, the protagonist tells a strange love story in a mischievous tone that plays with the absurdity of time and space.

Finally, it might be worth mentioning that two of the stories have been written directly in English (Fadwa al-Qasem's and mine), while the other eight have been wonderfully translated from their original languages by a group of talented translators, to whom I'd like to pay a well-deserved tribute at this point. I am deeply grateful for all their efforts and commitment, which helped immensely in bringing the needed element of harmony to this anthology.

★

Back to the top, in the same to-and-fro spirit of this book: if literature, as I have said, can fill the gap between people and civilizations, and I believe it can, it is evident on this level that, instead of insisting on the differences between East and West, we need to renew what we have in common. Instead of using the contrasts that exist between us as a source of discord, we need to invest in them in a way that makes *all of us* richer, on human, cultural and social levels.

Because if you come to think of it, we look a lot like each other, and our lives are not that different from yours. Furthermore, if you stare long enough in the mirror, I'm quite certain you'll see our eyes twinkling back at you.

We look a lot like each other, yet we are dissimilar. Not because you're from the West, and we are from the East. Not because you're a European, and we are Middle-Easterners. Not because you write from left to right, and we write from right to left. We are dissimilar, because all human beings on the face of the Earth are dissimilar. We are dissimilar, as much as you are dissimilar with your next door neighbour. This is what makes life interesting.

Do you really want to know 'us' better? Then start by believing there is no 'us'… There are no human samples, no stereotypes. Every person and every path in life are unique. Seek the nucleus, search for the individual. The whole is comprised in the core.

⋆

Last but not least, a necessary assertion of helplessness: I the undersigned hereby admit that I do not have answers to the pressing and frightening questions that are being asked worldwide in our time, regarding the dialogue of cultures and the so-called clash of civilisations (nor do I aspire to attain them one day). I am merely a writer (of the individualist sort, to make things even worse, if possible), whose almost only tool to understand the world, and to make it – sometimes – a better place has been, and will always be, books.

Yet, as a writer too, I am equally and genuinely convinced (dare I repeat it) that literature is one of the best ways to establish a true intercultural dialogue, to get past clichés, chimeras and fantasies. And by doing so, it holds the power to narrow the divides that exists between different people: an unpretentious, humble, power*less* − hence authentic, durable and efficient − kind of a power.

Therefore, I truly hope that this book, in addition to (i) being an enjoyable and inspiring read, (ii) introducing (in some cases, re-introducing) amazing writers from the region to English readers, and (iii) expressing my chronic passion for good literature, I hope it will also represent as well − in a 'collateral benefit' kind of a way that would not harm the gratuitousness of its fervently literary aspiration − one step forward in that seemingly impossible direction.

Joumana Haddad
Beirut, September 2008

The Award

NEDIM GÜRSEL

Yesterday I gazed at you from a hilltop, beloved Istanbul.

As the fog recedes, the city discloses itself. Ash-colored domes, the Beyazit Tower, thin as a thread. The opposite shore not yet visible. Üsküdar held in hazy emptiness. So, too, the Maiden's Tower, enveloped in the mist rising from the sea, a dusky-white apparition barely discernible in the distance. The red blinker on its steeple, now on now off. As the fog recedes, buildings, trees, roads emerge into view. The morning's first buses, the first passengers, the first ferry's smoke. He knows that the new day will also awaken the hum of the city. Persistent, strange, maddening to the unaccustomed ear. A river will run, beating against the levees. A battered bus will take the hill, always in second gear.

For years this hum did not cease or abate, even when the city's silhouette began to fade from his mind, the straight lines and curves began converging into one another, even when the blue of the sea and the green of the sycamores, the white of the ancient city walls and of the stone buildings began dissolving, disappearing in opaque colorlessness like the turbid waters of the Golden Horn. When the sun rose over the Parisian rooftops, he heard the sounds of his childhood. The glass-clear voice of the water vendor, the tired voice of the

1

peddler. What woke him up in the middle of the night were the muted horns of the ferries crossing the Bosphorus, not the drone of the Glacière metro.

Yesterday I gazed at you from a hilltop, beloved Istanbul. So he returned in the end. Like the last Ottoman poet, he is gazing at Istanbul from above. From the balcony of his room in the city's tallest hotel. With the fog receding, the September sun reflects off the sea, the fidgety waves, the seagulls, the white frames of ships anchored at the harbor. There, Kubbealti and the luxuriant gardens of Topkapi, the ugly public park in Sarayburnu, the magnificent dome of Aya Sofia. Just across, the javelin-like minarets of Sultanahmet. There, the Golden Horn, further out, the Suleymaniye Mosque. The doves of the New Mosque, the crowds on the Galata Bridge. Here, the city he spent a life away from, here, endless separation.

'Separation never ends,' he thinks to himself. A tired cliché but it says so much. Especially if you've reached the age of wisdom. Fortunately he doesn't depend on trite sayings and arabesque songs for inspiration. He isn't yet fully attuned to the public's sensibilities. Unlike other authors of his generation, he doesn't fashion story titles out of *endless separations* or *dusks at the harbour of longing*. At the same time, it is true that separation never ends altogether, that longing never dies away. *Wounded with longing. Age of wisdom. The past is a wound in my heart.* All of them wonderful, especially this last one. How many titles it has engendered, but so what! It's true, the past is a wound in people's hearts, embers in their bosom. *Ah, Soul, either die in love, or of desire!* Every so often, verses like these, odd bits of song lyrics pop into his mind. *Away for years from Istanbul, I am worn out with longing / I have no room left for dreams.* Instead of crafting elegant descriptions full of symmetrical, perfectly-pitched sentences, or dishing up meticulously detailed lovemaking scenes that would delight his readers, especially his female readers – the kind of writing that the literary critics no longer find interesting yet the young intellectuals enjoy and, with each passing day, embrace as their own – instead of these, his pen comes up with slapdash, second-hand phrases. No doubt the award wasn't given to him on account of his random musings. It was in recognition of the first work of an author who had known the sorrows of exile, and 'expressed in an authentic and innovative voice the tragedy of his generation, the crisis of young intellectuals during the military regime, the irremediable wounds of a period of oppression.'

Yesterday, when they picked him up at the airport, the director of the national academy issuing the award gave a televised press conference, recommending his book as a must-read for younger generations who ought to learn the lessons of the past. When it was his turn to speak, he simply expressed his 'happiness for being back in Istanbul after all these years,' and, all of a sudden, blurted out, 'Separation never ends.' 'It ne-e-e-ver ends, this se-e-e-paration / this wou-ou-ou-ound of lo-o-o-onging!' Pretending not to have heard this mock and entirely unwelcome singing, they edited it out of the TV broadcast. He was, after all, the recipient of the nation's most prestigious literary award, and a renowned author overseas. Perhaps he had wanted to express his homesickness, the pain of *lost years* with a little bit of humor. Worried that he might begin singing next, *If they gave me back my lost years*, the officials interrupted the press conference, hurried him into a car and dropped him off here, at the hotel with the most panoramic view of the city.

No one, not a single person came to check on him at dinner. The cocktail reception planned in his honor was cancelled, the new editions of his book were held at the printer. Now he is standing on the balcony, gazing at the city while the morning sun breaks through the fog and the first rays of daylight caress his sleepless face. He sees himself holding his mother's hand, getting on the Üsküdar ferry. Wearing a pair of shorts, polished shoes and a black suit, how serious he looks. They are on their way to visit his father's grave. Soon his mother will recite the *Fatiha* prayer while he gives himself to the coolness of the cypresses rustling in the breeze. A voice that feels both distant and near, very near, will whisper in his ear the lines from an old ballad that he would keep hearing for years and one day use as the opening lines of a story that he would begin writing while sitting at a cafe at Place de la Sorbonne, a story he could never finish:

Tap, tap, my pumpkin sweet
Gone and left me, my daddy sweet

He sees himself reading a book in the shadow of a sycamore, in the backyard of Galatasaray Lycée. Soon it will be evening. In the dormitory, he must settle for the pale blue light of the night lamp to continue his enchanting journey with words. Now he sees himself in Kuledibi, descending the street of brothels, as if descending into a well. His face pockmarked with acne, his gaze clouded. His school bag in hand, his palms sticky with sweat. In a Beyazit café, the same hands hold those of a girl with fair skin and blue eyes. And on that evening, while the police raid the dormitory of Istanbul Technical University and kill Vedat Demircioglu – *They shot Demircioglu Vedat, the son of ironsmiths, they killed him!* – he gets to taste the first passion on a satin couch in an attic apartment. The first elation of lovemaking with a woman without paying her. The first pain. The first separation. Just like his first brush with death at Taksim Square.

The march had begun in front of the university. The crowd had descended like an avalanche from the Beyazit Square to Cagaloglu, an avalanche that grew more immense as it rolled down, crossing the police barricade guarding the bridge, and arriving in Dolmabahçe. He remembers chanting songs of liberation at the vessels of the U.S. Sixth Fleet anchored on the Bosphorus. *Young they were, perhaps you've seen them / They wanted freedom, freedom they sang!* Afterwards, the marchers had climbed the hill to Taksim Square. He was in the front row. Next to him, the girl with the fair skin and blue eyes. They were holding hands. In Taksim Square, the police had penetrated the crowd, encircling the thousand or so marching in the front rows, pushing them toward the counter-demonstrators waiting for them, with clubs and rocks in hand, near the Taksim Park. He remembers losing sight of his first girlfriend in the panic, witnessing his friends being stabbed while the police watched, running for his life and hiding in the basement of a building. Yes, years later, standing one morning on the balcony of the Etap Marmara Hotel, he remembers Bloody Sunday. And standing where he does, he cannot see Taksim Square.

Besides, he always remembered what he could not see – more precisely, what he had once seen but forgotten. For years he kept Istanbul alive in his memory. The friends untimely lost, as well, those he left behind. Now, as he follows the city's rhythms below, the crowded sunny streets descending to the sea, the dark facades of the buildings caught in the endless hum, his mind gets caught in the tangle of the things he had not seen for years and would never see again. The perished Tarlabasi district with its hundred year old buildings, the ramshackle houses along the Golden Horn, the narrow streets, the Marquis Patisserie, its four beautifully tiled wall panels, the female figures with fiery hair depicting the four seasons. One time around noon, he was sitting in a Köprüalti tavern with some friends who are no longer alive, drinking *karafaki raki* in the August heat, and watching the hulks rotting along the Golden Horn; a boat had appeared out of nowhere, docking at the port in Persembepazari, and the boatman had leapt ashore, frantically screaming at the crowd, 'Alas, all that will happen, all the things!' 'Fires! Fires! There will be fires!' The police had grabbed the poor man at the cuffs and collar, scurried him to jail or the asylum, to give him a lashing and silence him for good. But, alas, the things that did happen. All the fires, all the destruction! That Köprüalti tavern is no more.

Persembepazari gone. Shores filled with concrete; beautiful buildings razed to the ground; green spaces, once the site of ancient Byzantine cisterns, now turned into landfills heaped with construction waste; storied waterfront mansions hemmed in by the 'staked' road built just off the Arnavutköy shoreline that, standing on the balcony, he cannot see − all this he had read in the newspapers, learned everything even before he had set foot in Istanbul. Everything that happened and did not happen! The wound of longing for lost things! That's indeed what he wanted to scream about at the press conference. The ashes from a fire were in reality the dust and detritus of an unimaginable destruction never before witnessed. *Ashes from a fire.* There was a song that began with these words. Zeki Müren used to sing it the best, yes, ashes from a fire.

Errant song lyrics begin whizzing through his head again. To escape the visions, the nightmares of the past that have laid siege to his mind, to be left alone with Istanbul, even if for a moment, he tries to remember the night before, the real award the city gave him.

It was near midnight when the phone had rang.

'You have a visitor, sir.'

'At this hour?'

'A lady. She insists on seeing you.'

'Fine, let her come upstairs.'

He sensed it from the way she tapped on the door. Anxiously, reluctantly. With her blue gaze, she had left the Istanbul night and came to stand before him. Under her décolleté dress, she was nearly naked. With her delicate mouth, her short hair, her moist lips, she looked just the way she did when they had first met. The years had not passed, time had not elapsed. They held hands. Separation had not come in between them, death had not come calling for the young.

'I saw you on the television. Congratulations.'

'...'

'The right choice. It was your best book. Too bad you

6

write different stuff now.'

He kissed first on her quivering lips, then her hair. After so many years, he embraced the award he earned by the power of his pen, and held it pressed against his chest until the morning. Alone now, without expectation, he gazes at the beloved Istanbul from above. And he sees not one place he has visited or loved.

Translated from the Turkish by Aron R. Aji

LIVERPOOL JOHN MOORES UNIVERSITY
LEARNING SERVICES

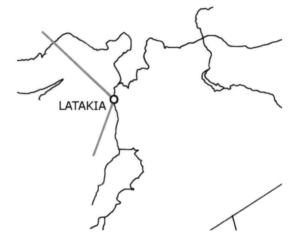

LATAKIA

City of Crimson

NABIL SULAYMAN

Wasif stood on the balcony, looking on impassively as the nursery bus took Thuraya away: Isn't she your daughter, you good-for-nothing?

No sooner had the bus disappeared from view than Ramziya went rushing off in the opposite direction on her way to the Department – the Department of Health. And no sooner had Ramziya disappeared from view than Wasif took a deep breath, then went dashing up the broad, ancient staircase that joined earth and sky: Isn't she your wife, you good-for-nothing?

On the foothill, that is, on the fortress's cheek, as Wasif liked to call it, there stood fifty-four steps that led from the street to the spacious, old, stately house Ramziya had inherited from her father, and which she'd come to live in with Wasif on their wedding night.

Beyond the house, the foothill ascended hurriedly in grassy verdure until it reached the Maghribi Shrine with its mosque and graveyard. It was there that, every morning, Wasif would turn into a spinning top, twirling about and embracing the sea from all directions. At the same time, he would find himself embraced by the hill, the barrack and the remaining trees, thorns and sparrows. However, from the time he'd come to believe that Latakia was safe no longer – that is, from the time he'd first seen it stained with crimson one morning in some forgotten month (April, perhaps) of some forgotten year (1980, perhaps) – he had abandoned his morning tradition.

The city had awakened to a pouring rain, and the path Wasif had to climb to the Maghribi hill, or the fortress hill, was muddy, so he was late coming out. From the middle of Maliki Street he veered toward the Ugarit Square and saw the Roman columns bathing blissfully in the downpour. Having arrived at the home of his friend, Dr. Abd al-Rahman Hilal, he knocked exuberantly on the door. To his surprise, however, the door was opened by his friend's Bulgarian wife, who informed him that the doctor had gone to the clinic an hour earlier.

What? Thought Wasif: did I see her in a dream?

Wasif decided to go on loitering in the rain, since it wouldn't matter to anyone if he arrived at the Feed Department at the beginning of the work day or at the end of it. And when, after the rain had begun to subside, he realized he was in front of the Health Department, he sought out Ramziya who, along with the other ladies that worked with her, was appalled to find him so wet. When he mentioned Abd al-Rahman, she said she'd seen him coming out of the Arif Bookstore and had waved to him, but that he hadn't seen her.

Then, as Wasif was waving goodbye to her at the end of the corridor, a voice screamed in terror, 'They've murdered Dr. Abd al-Rahman Hilal!'

'They've murdered who, you crazy woman?'

Wasif may have been the last one to scream, just as he had been the last one to believe that a young man or two – what was the difference, even if there had been ten of them? – had been following the doctor, who had come and opened the clinic early before the nurse arrived. Then suddenly there had been the sound of gunfire. And what difference did it make whether there had been one bullet, or a hundred? All that mattered was that the murderer had sauntered out, leaving Abd al-Rahman to bleed to death before the nurse arrived.

★

The crimson morning, or Abd al-Rahman's morning: that was what Wasif had come to call it. And morning after morning, he'd become addicted to recalling what Abd al-Rahman had taught his friends, both male and female, from the time they were little children gathered about him at the site of the ancient Ugarit.[1] He would mount a stone in one of its corners or immerse his bare feet in the wet sand. Then, in a voice as soft as the waves' gentle murmurs, he would say, 'This is where the grape press was, and over there was the olive press. Here was the blacksmith, and there was the smelter.'

'And over there,' he added, stretching out his arm toward the most distant wave, 'was the fisherman and his net. And the bait was a crab, Wasif.'

This was how Wasif had learned to open up the crab's gland and pick up its iron particles. However, Abd al-Rahman had waited until after he died to teach Wasif alone of all his friends how to sail from the Ibn Hani Cape with whatever fishermen he happened to meet. He had taught him how to wait patiently until they were weighed down with loads of mollusks of every shape and kind. He had taught him not to leave the workers while they were pressing the loads, after which they would salt the juice for three days and nights, then leave it on a low fire for ten days and nights. They would promise Wasif a cask brimming with crimson. However, he wasn't going to dye a silk dress for Ramziya or a woolen blanket for Abd al-Rahman's widow. Instead, he was going to sprinkle Latakiya's morning with blood. Then it would harbor the fear of assassination and be split into factions and sects, bidding farewell to safety as the blood and the crimson were reduced to one.

★

1. Ugarit – now known as Ras Shamra, was an ancient cosmopolitan port city situated north of Latakia, and was rediscovered in 1928. At the height of its polity (between 1450 and 1200 BC), it traded with Egypt and Cyprus and developed one of the world's oldest alphabets.

It was through these things that Wasif had become intolerable: silent and angry day and night. Ramziya had become addicted to reproaching him fearfully and blaming him for his self-imposed isolation, since he never left his room anymore except in the morning. And when he did, it wasn't to climb to the top of the hill and embrace the sea. Rather, it was to count the steps from the upper end of Maliki Street as he was doing now, then forget to count as soon as he was across from the tumbledown, cupolaed door that concealed the Armenian School. From in front of the bakery that still used firewood to bake its bread, Wasif would go back to counting again until he reached the church. Then he would remember − it may have been every morning that he remembered − that this was where he had welcomed in the New Year with Ramziya when they were still sweethearts. They had happened to meet Abd al-Rahman at the church door, where they had exchanged hugs, kisses and animated conversation.

After pronouncing his blessing on the two Muslim lovers' choice of the church as their rendezvous site, Abd al-Rahman had asked Ramziya, 'Whose church is this, Miss Smarty?'

'It's the Roman Catholic Church, doctor,' she rejoined hurriedly.

'Wrong, Miss Smarty,' he replied with a reproachful tweak on her ear.

Then, turning to Wasif he said, 'And you, Mr. Smarty, whose church is this?'

'It's the Saint Nicolas Church,' came the reply.

'Good for you!' said Abd al-Rahman, rewarding Wasif by tweaking his ear, too.

Then he disappeared into the holiday crowd, leaving Wasif's eyes searching for him just as they were doing now. He got as far as the Ahram Cinema, and when he despaired anew of finding Abd al-Rahman either alive or dead, he crossed over to the sidewalk in front of the Kindi Cinema, feeling torn and besieged between the messages proclaimed by this cinema and that. He charged ahead until Maliki Street had led him to the park: but why was it dry and barren?

The corniche, too, had turned desolate both morning and evening, not only because the city was no longer safe by day or by night, but, rather, because the expansion of the port had distanced the sea from the corniche, as a result of which it was no longer filled with flocks of young women every afternoon, both summer and winter. However, the corniche continued to be a refuge for those who, male and female alike, came to escape from the schools and the fledgling university and loiter here the way Wasif was doing now. Just then, though, he was accosted by one of the cars that had so proliferated in the city since Dr. Abd al-Rahman Hilal's assassination. Wasif had memorized its appearance by now: a Land Rover, that is, a patrol car. What difference did it make if it was a patrol from military security, political security, state security or something else? Whatever it happened to be, Wasif would leave the corniche post haste and lose himself among the alleyways, taking care to steer clear of the streets until he had no choice but to cross the last of them on his way to the Farous Cemetery. Once he found himself in front of the cemetery, he would be standing under the balcony from which Ramziya used to peer down on her admirers: How did you alone manage to win her, you good-for-nothing?

*

Ramziya's elderly father was surprised to receive a visit from Wasif, who had rarely darkened his father-in-law's door, particularly since the death of Ramziya's mother. To Wasif's surprise, the old man didn't complain of loneliness or grumble over the insubordination of his sons and daughters, first and foremost, Ramziya. Perhaps that was what helped Wasif relax in the sitting room that opened out onto the graveyard. Although he had his eyes closed, he could see the elderly man gesturing against the background of the tombstones. Meanwhile, his voice carried on with a melancholy litany whose beginning no one recalled and whose end no one could predict:

'Nothing's left of the Farous Monastery.[2] That's right. But people built the monastery after the liberation. Salah al-Din's[3] soldiers built it, too.'

'Soldiers destroyed all of Latakia,' said Wasif peevishly. 'What do you mean, they built this or that?'

The old man's arm went limp and he pursed his lips, and Wasif felt sorry for him. In order to vent his anger, he had begun glorifying the hero that had liberated Latakia from the Europeans, while forgiving the soldiers who had destroyed Roman columns, panels, and marble stones, then carried away to Damascus whatever they hadn't destroyed.

The two men were seated across from each other on the house's sole, antique sofas. With difficulty Wasif parted his eyelids as the old man asked scornfully, 'Do you know where al-Ma'arri[4] learned Greek philosophy, Professor Wasif? Right here, my dear son-in-law. Here, at the Farous Monastery. This cemetery bears witness to it. But what would *you* know?'

Wasif replied sardonically, 'I know your city drove al-Ma'arri mad, with church bells ringing on one side, and someone shouting from a minaret on the other.'

Starting at Wasif's comment, the old man bellowed, 'Never in its history did Latakia know divisions until *your* generation!'

2. Farous Monastery – described by the 14th century traveler Ibn Battuta as the greatest monastery in the Levant and Egypt combined. Thought to have flourished under Mamluke rule during the fourteenth century AC; however, it was destroyed during the great earthquake which struck Latakia in 1469 AC.
3. Salah al-Din - better known as 'Saladin' in medieval Europe, Salah al-Din Ayyoubi (d. 1193) was a Sultan of Egypt and Syria and led the Islamic opposition to the Third Crusade.
4. Abul'Ala' al-Ma'arri (d. 1057 AC) – renowned Arab poet known for his scepticism, rationalism and humanistic vision. Born in Ma'arrat al-Nu'man near Aleppo, Syria.

Indignant, Wasif closed his eyelids again. And as though his eyelids had been infected with the old man's mental disarray, they began to play on his imagination: flying him away to the cemetery with Ramziya's father, stuffing the old man inside a grave alongside his wife, digging up the graves one and all and sending their residents to the sea, then turning the graveyard back into the free, colorful, open space it had once been before Salah al-Din Ayyoubi had liberated the city, or before it had been buried beneath the outpourings of a volcano. Wasif fancied the idea of bringing Ramziya's father together with Abul-'Ala' al-Ma'arri some day in the tourist casino and summer resort, and some other day, with al-Mutanabbi[5] at the Blue Beach Resort. He imagined building pretty little houses around the monastery and revitalizing the Farous neighborhood. Ramziya had looked down from this balcony on her admirers, and Wasif could hardly have won her if it hadn't been for the fact that the earth was shaken by a mighty convulsion.

Then the voice of Ramziya's father came again, carrying on with a melancholy litany whose beginning no one recalled and whose end no one could predict:

'Nothing's left of Latakia. The houses have turned into graves. And the survivors have sought refuge in the orchards.'

When did that happen? Wasif wondered to himself.

And because the old man's ears were so good he could have heard a needle drop in a haystack, he said, 'Around this same time of the year, in late April two hundred years ago.'

'Less than that,' muttered Wasif sarcastically.

'A little less,' Ramziya's father replied indifferently. 'And in the orchards it was rumored that bigger earthquakes were to follow, so the people went rushing into the rubble and brought back with them whatever livestock had survived and whatever possessions they could gather. Then they hurried

---

5. Al-Mutanabbi (d. 965 AC) – 10th century court poet known for his egotism and grandiosity; his name means 'he who claims to be a prophet'.

away as far as they could get.'

'To the sea?' asked Wasif with feigned stupidity, whereupon Ramziya's father went on derisively, 'No, to the villages, Mr. Know-it-all. They set up tents in the wilderness, Mr. Know-it-all. Then they waited. But God was merciful to them and there wasn't another earthquake.'

'Thirty years later there was,' Wasif added knowingly.

'A little less than that,' mumbled the old man drowsily. 'But thirty years after the earthquake, the plague broke out. That's right.'

Before long he had fallen completely silent as though he were fast asleep, or as though he had died peacefully. That was what Wasif guessed, at any rate – or perhaps he just wished it – as he slipped out of the house.

★

By the time Wasif reached home, the sky had cleared so completely you would have thought it hadn't rained for an entire month, and the sunset adorned the heavenly expanse with an enchanting array of colors. Even so, he was worn out and dejected.

He had spent the remainder of his day going about as though he were inspecting the city or bidding it farewell. Sometimes the city would appear to him as though it were on the verge of some catastrophe, and at others, it would seem to be just emerging from one. Perhaps this was why he made his first stop at the Ja'far al-Sadiq Mosque,[6] then passed by the Protestant Church, followed by the Abu al-Darda' Mosque, the Uwaynah Mosque, the Armenian Church, the Amshati Mosque, the Maronite Church, and the Port Mosque. At this last point Wasif took a longer rest, as he did also at the Umm

---

6. Ja'far al-Sadiq (d. 765 AC) – believed by the Twelver and Ismaili Shi'ite Muslims to be the sixth infallible imam, or spiritual leader and successor to the Prophet Muhammad.

al-Sultan Shrine.[7] However, with every place he stopped, he felt more confused than he had at the one before. Hunger, along with a vague sense of alienation, may have exacerbated the state he was in, and this despite the greetings he had exchanged with those he had chanced to pass by, male and female alike. Finally he broke down and ate a falafel sandwich from Al-Hamawi the way Abd al-Rahman Hilal used to do whenever he had the chance, even after becoming Latakia's number one neurologist.

After stopping at al-Hamawi, Wasif's shadow became one with Abd al-Rahman: a dead man raised to life, and a living man raised to death. As such, everything turned hazy for both friends, each of whom looked upon the other as the sacrifice that was to be slaughtered right here, a stone's throw away, in some corner of Ugarit. So let one of them be a boy child, and the other a girl: what difference would it make so long as the sacrifice was going to be daubed with plaster and lay wrapped in a vault?

Even so, Wasif hoped he wouldn't be placed in the sarcophagus, and if that wasn't possible, he hoped the sarcophagus wouldn't be lowered into the grave. Let that be Abd al-Rahman's prerogative, not only because he had been the first to die, but because he had taken such pride in his Phoenician ancestor, and because it was that ancestor who had established such customs in relation to sacrifices. The person who had killed Abd al-Rahman may also have done so in 'recompense' for his Phoenician-ness, and not only because – as had been rumored throughout Latakia on the morning of crimson or the morning of Abd al-Rahman – he had been a Communist or an Alawite: What do you think, Ramziya?

★

7. Umm al-Sultan Sha'ban – a woman famed for her charity and generosity. When she went on the pilgrimage to Mecca in 1359 AC, she is said to have taken with her one hundred royal mamlukes, musicians, and camels laden with merchandise.

When Wasif reached home, this question was the only thing that passed his lips. With a disapproving look, Ramziya rushed to Thuraya's room. For the first time, he went to bed early, and may have gone to sleep before Thuraya did. And for the first time, Wasif was up before dawn. He woke with a start, his heart beating wildly. However, he calmed down quickly, and was left with the feeling that someone had been tickling him. The man smiled as coarse fingers made their way stealthily toward his eyelids, then began rubbing fiercely. The smile itself felt ticklish, and he moved his head about uneasily in an attempt to escape from the fingers, which had grown coarser and rougher than ever. Then all of a sudden, his ears were pierced with the sound of a bullet whizzing through the air. No, three bullets. No, a shower of them: a shower of bullets that came pouring down like rain. Then no less suddenly, the spray of bullets thinned out, and silence reigned. Meanwhile, the bed had rolled Wasif into a ball, frozen him in place and made his mouth go dry.

He might have stayed that way till Resurrection Day had it not been for the fact that Ramziya charged into the room, saying in a terrified voice,

'The world's going to pot and you're asleep?!'

'What's going on?!' he asked in a voice even more terrified.

Then he began shouting out things he couldn't make sense of any more than he'd made sense of what Ramziya had said. However, when Ramziya charged in and dawn's cool breezes wafted through the room, he realized that the bullets had begun flying again, though this time they were like hail. And this time they were far from this safe house, in this safe neighborhood, in this... city.

Has Latakia really become unsafe? he wondered as he went scuffling toward the balcony. When his shoulder was up against Ramziya's and warmth flowed through the forearms that had happened to come into contact, he wished her bed were back in the room once more. Wasif felt a vague tremor that quickly gave way to fear even though the gunfire had begun to die down. However, Ramziya's torso, which had also happened to touch Wasif's, turned the fear into desire. The desire waited until the silence had grown complete, at which point Wasif wrapped his arm around Ramziya's waist.

'Scared?' he whispered.

'Are you?' she whispered back with a lustiness that caused her arms to wrap themselves around Wasif's neck, then bury his face between her breasts. For the first time in the eleven years they'd been married, her lips were the first to go searching for his, and her fingers weren't too shy to come after his organ. And, also for the first time since they had married, his organ exploded in Ramziya's grip as she rubbed him with vigor and relish. Perhaps it hadn't been mockery or revenge, but simple curiosity. Whatever it was, the rubbing had made Wasif grind his teeth and caused his breathing to become painful as his organ went limp as a rag.

★

No sooner had the gunfire begun reverberating again in the safe city's dawn than Wasif's whole being went limp as a rag. Ramziya left the balcony and he escorted her out, grateful to the Almighty that she'd left him the room to himself and moved her bed into Thuraya's room since she wasn't able to walk straight yet: so why had he been wishing she would move her bed back into this room, which had begun quaking from the force of the gunfire?

No, no. It isn't gunfire. It's, at the very least, a bomb that's pounding the dawn of this city that's safe no longer. Thus thought Wasif to himself as he went catapulting into the room, which then catapulted him into the living room. Thuraya rubbed her eyes and yawned, then cast her father a dispassionate glance. He was treated to a similar glance by Ramziya as she emerged with a small suitcase and even smaller bag in her hand.

'We'll be at my family's house,' she announced sullenly.

So, all that had happened the day before. Today, however, Wasif had awakened to tranquil silence, dazzling light, and blessed solitude: with no wife, no daughter, no bullet, no bomb, and no Latakia.

Having washed his hands of everything, he went flitting back and forth between the bed, the bathroom, the cup of coffee, the kitchen window, the closet, the stairs, and the entrance to the building, which opened wide like a loosely packed grave about to spit out its trifling contents. In other words, it was about to eject this man onto Maliki Street the way it had ejected him the day before. However, not at such an early hour or with such lightness of heart: Are you really happy to see Ramziya and Thuraya go, you good-for-nothing?

Yes, sir, I'm happy and then some! His steps were jaunty and assured. And as he clenched his fist, it added: Ramziya's family's house is safer than this one, the Farous neighborhood is safer than the Qal'ah neighborhood, and the Qal'ah neighborhood is safer than the Raml neighborhood. In fact, the Raml neighborhood is safer than the Salibiyah neighborhood.

And as long as all of Latakia could boast of such safety, what had happened the day before hadn't really happened: But what are you bragging about, you good-for-nothing?

*

The question continued to eat away at Wasif, causing him to turn this way and that as he made his way down Maliki Street, crossing one alley after another until the Joul Jammal Secondary School came into view. Through the students' loud clamor, Wasif seemed to hear his elderly father-in-law's voice drawing steadily nearer.

'This is where I studied,' he said boastfully. 'I was in the *prouvé*, which is what you call the secondary school diploma these days. That was when Hafez Asad and Adonis were in university.'

The old man's voice turned into a tender echo when he remembered that this school had borne the name of Joul Jammal[8] when he was a university student.

'After all,' muttered Wasif, 'Joul Jammal was a hero, and he deserved it.' This was what Abd al-Rahman Hilal had said whenever he recalled Joul Jammal. Abd al-Rahman was also fond of saying that Joul Jammal had been stained with crimson as befits a Phoenician. And sometimes, out of deference for Wasif, he would add, 'And as befits a Latakian.' As Wasif approached the Alexandria Café, he thought about the fact that what Joul and Abd al-Rahman had been stained with was blood: the first in the sea, and the second in his clinic, the first as he fought to repel the French barge off the shores of Egypt, and the second as he fought to repel... to repel whom from Syria?

The question had kept Wasif awake for nights on end ever since that morning, the morning he now referred to as the morning of crimson, or the morning of Abd al-Rahman. Sometimes the answer would break through to him as: the Muslim Brotherhood. Other times it would be: the intelligence bureau, and still others, Saddam Hussein's agents. In the end, though, the answer took a single form, namely: the people Abd al-Rahman Hilal had been fighting to drive out of Syria were simply the people who murdered him. And at that point the question had fallen fast asleep and hadn't wakened again until the day before, just like Wasif himself, who had been fast asleep until he was wakened shortly after 9am by a tearful Thuraya, who said, 'Baba, the bus didn't come.'

---

8. Joul Jammal – a native of Latakia, and naval officer under Egypt's President Nasser, lead a naval operation involving torpedo boats against a French destroyer, during the Suez Crisis (also known as the Tripartite Aggression) of 1956, and was killed in the process, thereby going down in history as a model of heroism.

So, then, Thuraya wouldn't be going to the nursery school, and Wasif would have to take care of her until Ramziya returned from the department – the Department of Health – six hours later. However, Ramziya returned six minutes later roaring, 'The streets are closed, Wasif! No taxis, and no buses. I was afraid for them to take Thuraya to the nursery school, and I thought to myself: if you go, sweetheart, how will you get home again? I tried to get to the Department, but I couldn't, Wasif. They're saying, "God have mercy on Sheikh Yousef Sarim[9]."'

'So what's that supposed to mean?' Wasif asked irritably.

She shot him a furious look, then went on roaring, 'What's that supposed to mean? It means they murdered him the way they murdered Abd al-Rahman. That's it. Latakia has gone to pot just like Hama and Aleppo. All of Syria's become like Lebanon now. Don't forget how they used to say about Sheikh Yousef Alawi, 'He's the imam,' and, 'He's the muezzin', and 'The mosque belongs to Ja'far al-Sadiq, to the Alawites and the Shi'ites.' So, do you know what it means now, or do I need to explain it further?'

Ignoring his wife's sarcasm, Wasif kept still until Ramziya and Thuraya had left. Once they were gone, though, he charged like a mad bull from the door of the flat to the entrance of the building, which hadn't come to resemble the mouth of a tomb yet. From the entrance of the building he made his way up fifty-four steps which he wasn't going to count this time, and from the steps to the street. However, no sooner did he find himself halfway across it than he got the feeling someone was following him, and was going to catch up with him within another step or two. It was as though Wasif Imran – the mathematics teacher who, after Abd al-Rahman Hilal's assassination, had been transferred to the

---

9. Sheikh Yousef al-Sarim – an Alawite and one of Latakia's religious leaders in the 70s. Despite his strong Sunnite leanings, he was assassinated in 1979 by the Muslim Brotherhood amid accusations that Alawites were not true Muslims.

Feed Department because the intelligence bureau had classified him as a member of the opposition – were the one who had murdered Sheikh Yousef Sarim. Obsessive thoughts began to assail him:

'Did you shoot the poor man, or did you stab him with a knife?'

'I did both, sir.'

'Describe for us what you did.'

'I lay in wait for the sheikh in front of his house, sir. And when he came out to deliver the call to prayer I shouted, 'Take that!' He got one bullet in his forehead, a second one slightly below the first, and a third in his navel.'

'What then, you criminal? What else did you do?'

'Then we set up an ambush in front of the mosque, sir. As usual, the sheikh came out early for fear that someone else would lead the prayer in his place. So I shouted at him, 'Take that!' Then I inflicted a single gaping wound that was enough to finish him off, sir.'

'Why, you criminal?'

Just then Wasif's ears were pierced by a scream that sent him leaping into the air like a monkey. Consequently, he escaped the rock that shattered the window of the car parked to his right, and he went rushing eastward with others who were heading the same direction. As they were on their way out of the city, he noticed that he looked rather out of place among all these young people. So he slowed his pace, and all of a sudden, a stick being wielded by one of the young men shattered the window of a car parked along the opposite sidewalk. No sooner had Wasif recovered from his stupor than the angry crowd of young men went lurching in the direction of a roundabout, which appeared in the distance to be choked with traffic.

Warily, he too approached the roundabout. When he reached it, he turned to look behind him as though he were bidding the city farewell. Just then he felt a shoulder shoving him and heard a voice prattling noisily, 'Curses on all your factions, the best and the worst alike. Hey you, you should be ashamed of yourselves! Hey you, fear God! Look, you've taken us back a hundred years! The days when the French ruled, the days when Turkey ruled – *those* were the days!'

The speaker then disappeared along with his voice, which was drowned out by the uproar in the roundabout, where hundreds of arms were raised high and brandishing clubs, cleavers, knives, whips, fists and daggers, all of them calling for revenge.

'What revenge, you lunatics?!' Wasif demanded, his chest about to burst.

By now the crowd had turned into an impenetrable wall. To the right, the street leading away from the roundabout was congested with traffic, while the cars were full to the brim with passengers since the taxi and bus stops had moved there. Seeing his stunned confusion, someone in the crowd offered to explain things to Wasif. As for Wasif, he was about to assure the man that what confused him was the people who filled the cars. However, the man disappeared. It occurred to Wasif that the city meant nothing to any of these people. Who knows? Maybe they'd never loved it in their entire lives. It may never have been anything to any of them but a tasty morsel, a woman with whom to satisfy their desires, a bank account, or a stream of blood gushing from the head of this young man in front of Wasif whom he could never forget: with his enormous, round, shaved head, his huge eyes and even huger ears, and a double-ended sword resembling Dhu al-Faqqar whose owner the young man was calling upon. The sword was so bright it blurred Wasif's vision. Then it blinded him entirely when it began passing rapidly over the young man's scalp. His scalp was stained bright red, and the blood spattered onto faces, heads and shirts. Veins in people's temples began to burst and pop in glorious revenge. But for whom, and against whom?

Wasif screamed. However, fear trapped the scream inside his chest, and thanks to the fear, his feet shuffled backwards until they had distanced themselves from the crowd. When they sensed they had reached safety, they sprinted in the direction of the Buqa roundabout, which was given its distinctive appearance by a set of towering round columns. His eyes longed for a glimpse of what they had burned into memory back in the days of his childhood, namely, the broken places among the columns' capitals and along their fallen lengths. However, a Land Rover crossed the roundabout and stopped in front of the sole unbroken column. The barrels of Kalashnikov rifles peeked out from inside the Jeep's windows. Wasif moved aside, and what should he find but more gun barrels protruding from the Jeep's back door. There seemed to have been some mistake. It may be that Wasif's fear turned into courage when the crowd began filling the roundabout. Consequently, he came forward in defiance of the patrol car, or in defiance of the crowd. In fact, fear may have overcome the patrol itself. Or it may have been a courage greater than Wasif's that caused someone in the crowd to defy the patrol. Whatever it was that happened, Wasif's ears were bombarded by the sound of a bullet. No, three bullets. No, a shower of them: a shower of bullets that came pouring down like rain, or perhaps like hail. Feeling reproachful and agitated, he turned his head, and what should he see but a radiant face approaching from the direction of the sea. The closer it came, the more it resembled the face of Abd al-Rahman. However, when it had situated itself directly across from Wasif, the person to whom the face belonged appeared to many to be carrying a huge cask brimming with crimson which he proceeded to pour out over Wasif, who had flung himself onto the pavement, vomiting blood.

Translated from the Arabic by Nancy Roberts

Living it Up (and Down) in Beirut

JOUMANA HADDAD

Act IV. No Smoke Without Fire (May 2008)

> *'Who, even in words not bound by meter,*
> *and having told the tale many times over,*
> *could tell the blood and wounds that I saw now?'*
>
> Dante, The Divine Comedy

'I have an erection,' said the woman whose green eyes make trees stumble.

'I have an erection too,' said the lover[1] of the woman whose green eyes make trees stumble.

It didn't occur to the man to ask the woman: 'How could you have an erection? You're a woman.'

That is exactly why he – a sailor whose blue tears

---

1. OPERATING MANUAL:
Allow me to inform you right from the start: This is not a love story. It might, at times, look a lot like a love story, but it's not. It's a story about a woman. About a woman's common sense. About a woman's fantasies. About a woman's foolish common sense, and totally rational fantasies. There will be a man too I guess. Men, even. And a city. An unwise, volcanic, Hara-Kiri kind of a city. And a loose bra strap that keeps falling down from a wild shoulder. There will also be nails in the story. Not necessarily long. Nor painted. But tough. Oh yes. And a football. There will definitely be a football. An old and dirty one. Revenge for my obsessive need to keep all possessions (things and people alike) as new and shiny as the first minute they became mine. *'Time to grow up. To accept the fact that stuff wears out'*. So my father used to say at least.

31

invented the Mediterranean Sea – was her lover. This is one of the numerous reasons why she liked him so much, she thought. And this is undoubtedly why he was lying naked by her side right now: because it would never occur to him to ask her dull questions like: 'How could you have an erection? You're a woman.'

She liked him as well because he, like her, was an austere, extinct kind of a hedonist, who loathed exclamation marks (mere juvenile plastic Kalashnikovs); pink (the stickiest color ever); nostalgia (at times a terrorist attack, at others an STD, depending on the idiocy of the situation); sugary words, actions and emotions (such meticulously nauseous and utterly inappropriate products); not to mention the itchiness that most people feel in the heart when they find out they've missed out on a well-deserved opportunity. What was it called again? Oh yes: self-pity. Yuck.

She also liked him, obviously, because he too had erections. Amazing ones. That was the cherry on top[2].

They met in Beirut on the 7th of May 2008[3]. He had arrived from Italy a few days earlier, as a guest of honor to the famous Hamra Poetry Festival, one of the city's annual literary events: an authentic, politically incorrect poet (the best breed), who combined the power of written verse with that of the spoken word. While she was listening to his breathtaking performance the evening before, at Masrah Al-Madina Theatre, she immediately noticed his hands and his voice. Two

---

2. Well, to be totally honest, it was more than just a 'cherry'.
3. The 2008 fighting in Lebanon began on May 7, after Lebanon's 17-month long political crisis spiraled out of control. The fighting was sparked by a government move to shut down Hezbollah's telecommunication network and remove Beirut Airport's security chief over ties to Hezbollah. Hezbollah leader Hassan Nasrallah said the government's decision to declare the group's military telecommunications network illegal was a 'declaration of war' on the organization, and demanded that the government revoke it. Then Hezbollah-led opposition fighters shut down the capital's international airport and seized control of several West Beirut neighborhoods, in street battles that left 11 dead and 30 wounded. It was the worst violence in Beirut since Lebanon's 1975-90 civil war. *(CNN.com)*

tired yet powerful hands, hands that have suffered intensely, but that are still capable of moving mountains, she knew intuitively; and a deep dominant voice, a majestic roaring voice, which woke the tamer that was in her, and left her feeling helpless at the same time.

So few, so refreshingly unlikely were the experiences that woke the tamer that was in her, and made her feel helpless simultaneously, that she couldn't but obsess over those hands and that voice – and the 50 year-old man that came with them – all night long. And since she was the (atypical) sort of a woman who, when she wanted something, would reach out and simply try to take it, instead of waiting for it to happen to her, she decided that she *had* to talk to Raffaele[4] the following morning. She *had* to shake one of those hands, let her thirsty palm touch that exhausted skin, a skin so drenched with stories to tell. She *had* to feel that voice wrap her in its potent texture and blazing tones, like wings of flesh and blood that would take her anywhere. Absolutely anywhere. And even though there was a serious strike in Beirut that day, a strike that was very likely to go very wrong[5], she headed nonetheless, around 9am, to the Bristol Hotel, located a few minutes away from her house.

Why am I doing this? she asked herself at one point almost amusingly. *I'm 37. I'm too old (and wise?) to follow a trail of smoke.*

No smoke without fire, she smartly auto-replied, then went inside the lobby, chose one of the red velvet comfortable sofas facing the elevator, and waited for him to appear.

---

4. Is this his real name, or am I bluffing you, dear readers, like almost any writer who respects him/herself?

5. I saw (1):

I saw a little girl lying amid rubble. Her name was Nour. Rouba was her name. It doesn't matter! Don't the dead children look alike in the deafening silence of their bodies? She liked rainbows and dreamt of becoming an astronaut. She finally rose to that sky that she had admired for so long from below. Nour: knight of the skies. Nour: astronaut of eternity.

And that was exactly what the poet/sailor whose blue tears invented the Mediterranean Sea, did...

Act I. No Rest for the Wicked (Jan 1990)

> *'Two events taking place at the points A and B of a system K are simultaneous if they appear at the same instant when observed from the middle point, M, of the interval AB. Time is then defined as the ensemble of the indications of similar clocks, at rest relatively to K, which register the same simultaneously'*
> Einstein, The Meaning of Relativity

Damn this country, she thought. *Damn this homicidal identity, damn this cruel geography, damn these nasty religions that turn man against man because of a god who is uncertain of his own existence...* She planted her dangerous nails[6] in the palms of her hands, one of several self-destructive practices she had picked up over the years – years of disenchantment, impatience and anger.

Conflict is my destiny, I need to accept it, she then said out loud in front of the mirror, repeatedly like a mantra, just to experience the hideous impact of such a statement on her ears, skin, lungs, stomach, pelvis, etc. In fact, she's been struck

---

6. Those dangerous nails are mine. I allowed my main character to borrow them *(she needed them badly, you see)*. But they are unquestionably mine.

Those dangerous nails are mine. They are the nails I write with. From those nails arise music, screams, whispers and roars that most people misleadingly call 'words'. From those nails start my verses and poems, my stories and my songs, and, at times, strange fairy-tales that always leave a trail of blood, of *my* blood, behind.

Yes, those dangerous nails are mine. Those are the nails I love with. Each scratch on a man's back, on a man's soul, is a cry of love, a cry for help *(what's the difference?)*. It is with those nails that I breathe, lick, kiss, and embrace. It is with those nails that I etch my shape on a memory, on a body, on a glimpse of what could have been, on a scent that never came by.

Those nails, those dangerous, poisonous, treacherous nails are mine. And so are the wounds, the dreadful wounds, the never healing wounds, the beloved, necessary wounds that come with them.

And that keep on crafting the geography of my life.

by the fatal lightning of war since she was four years old. It broke out in 1975. In April 1975. On the 13th of April 1975[7]. The 'Black Sunday', they call it. She revisited that tragic date in a flash and wondered sarcastically: *is 'fate' a pretext used by his Almightiness when he messes up? And why aren't we humans allowed to use it as well?*.

When they first heard the gun blasts and explosions that day, her parents thought they had to be fireworks. *Maybe it is some big shot's wedding,* her mother said, and kept on cooking the Sunday meal. But it wasn't some big shot's wedding. It was many big shots' war. A war that ate up the best years of her childhood and adolescence, a war that made her all rotten inside, full of putrid scars that she did her best to hide[8]. And here it was coming back again, uninvited yet quite resolute. So many innocent people were, once more, paying with their lives and hopes the price of a sin they did not commit, the scandalously high price of 'being Lebanese'. She felt so mad and frustrated...

She looked at her watch. It was only 13:00 hrs, yet it felt like ages since she woke up to the familiar sound of shells blowing up the Gemmayze neighborhood where she lived. It

7. The spark that ignited the civil war in Lebanon occurred in Beirut on April 13, 1975, when gunmen killed four Phalangists during an attempt on Pierre Jumayyil's life. Believing the assassins to have been Palestinian, the Phalangists retaliated later that day by attacking a bus carrying Palestinian passengers across a Christian neighborhood, killing about twenty-six of the occupants. The next day fighting erupted in earnest, with Phalangists pitted against Palestinian militiamen (thought by some observers to be from the Popular Front for the Liberation of Palestine). The confessional layout of Beirut's various quarters facilitated random killing. Most Beirutis stayed inside their homes during these early days of battle, and few imagined that the street fighting they were witnessing was the beginning of a war that was to devastate their city and divide the country for more than 16 years. *(Globalsecurity.org)*

8. I saw (2):

I saw a man weeping in front of his destroyed house. He was saying nothing, he was just weeping. He looked and wept, sitting on a heap of misshapen concrete that used to be his eldest son's room. The room disappeared. The eldest son too. The man's hand resting on his tears was quivering against his will. His defeated hand was learning how to abandon itself to its dark destiny. Devoured, tamed, the man's hand won't heal from its souvenirs.

was only 13:00 hrs, which can only mean, in a hellish time and place like these, that more people were still going to die that day, more houses were going to be destroyed, more children were going to become orphans and/or cadavers before night fell on the city...

At that moment, right out of the blue, amidst all the anger and desperation, the woman whose green eyes make trees stumble smiled, a strange smile that rose like a wild purple flower among ruins. She did not smile because she was slowly becoming insane. Nor did she smile because her heart was turning into stone[9]. She smiled because she remembered her lover, Raffaele[10]. They had met on the 31st of January 1990[11]. And it didn't matter at all that she was 19, and he was 32. He fit her like a glove.

She looked again. 13:06. Time seemed so heavy and thick, almost like mud. It was not flowing; it was rather rolling on her like huge rocks, and crashing her back again and again. She tried to ignore the intimidating explosions; it wasn't so difficult. She had become used to the symphony of combat... What a dreadful thing to say, feel and think. But it was true nevertheless. After so many years of training and alienation, she had become used to the symphony of combat, and to all the fear and death that came with it. 'I'm war-broken,' she would tell her foreign friends, in an attempt to make fun of what most hurt within her[12].

---

9. How she wished it did, at times.
10. They didn't really meet on the 7th of May 2008. They had actually met years before that.
11. On 31 January 1990, General Aoun's forces attacked positions of the Lebanese Forces (the Christian Militia) in East Beirut in an apparent attempt to remove the LF as a political force in the Christian enclave. In the heavy fighting that ensued in East Beirut and its environs, over 900 people died and over 3,000 were wounded. In October 1990, a joint Lebanese-Syrian military operation against General Aoun forced him to capitulate and take refuge in the French embassy. General Aoun remained in the French embassy until August 27 1991 when a 'special pardon' was issued, allowing him to leave Lebanon safely and take up residence in exile in France. (Almashriq.hiof.no)
12. Don't we all?

So she ignored the blasts and went back to her book. *L'italiano per gli stranieri.* She had decided to take up Italian lessons a few weeks ago, and managed to go to the institute for the first time on the same day that the Abolition War broke out between the Lebanese forces and the army led by General Michel Aoun. That was so like her: hopelessly gifted for interruption. For incomplete endeavors. It was almost a miracle she wasn't born missing a liver or a leg...

She felt extremely disappointed when the news of the battles suspended the first period, as she was keen to master this new language. First of all because she was passionate about languages, and convinced they were living beings, and deserved respect. Secondly, because she wanted to be able to read Cesare Pavese, one of her favorite poets, in his native idiom one day. And last but not least, because of Raffaele, her charming Italian teacher she had just met an hour ago. A professor who 'teaches to live, and writes poetry to survive,' he told the class when introducing himself. A professor so viciously dedicated to his job that he took her phone number on that unfinished first day, and promised to give her private lessons until the Italian cultural Institute opened its doors again. 'No rest for the wicked, I insist on teaching you,' he said to her, then broke down with laughter, the wettest laughter she has ever heard in her life. One that felt almost like a tongue between her thighs.

Another look at the watch: 13:56. Soon Raffaele would be arriving at her house for their daily afternoon class, and she was nervously looking out the bedroom window, trying to spot his black Mazda from afar. Why was she so tense? *Could it be love?* She let herself slip towards that cliffy thought for a second. But she quickly swept the absurd idea away[13], and waited for him to appear.

---

13. FOREWARNING:
Again, this is NOT a love story. It might, at times, look like one, but it's not. You have to believe me. It's rather a story about a woman, a city and a set of nails.

And that was exactly what the poet/teacher/sailor whose blue tears invented the Mediterranean Sea, did…

Act III. None so Blind as Those who will Not See (Jul 2006)

> 'This life as you now live it and have lived it, you will have to live innumerable times more. The eternal hourglass of existence is turned over and over, and you with it, a grain of dust.'
> Nietzsche, Joyful Science

She opened the blue wooden shades and all the noises and smells of the beach blew into her at once. Sharp, luscious and moist.

She had dreamt of this house for so long. A house right by the seaside, overlooking the famous corniche and the Rawcheh Rocks, near the AUB. As a child she used to say to her friends: 'One day, I will have a white house with windows that look like endless skies even when they're closed.'

Indeed, she had dreamt of this house for a very long time. Well, not this house in particular. But of a house, of almost any house, by the beach. Getting to buy one in the Rawcheh area was not exactly the way she imagined her fantasy would eventually turn out. She grew up as a Christian in a war-torn Beirut, and a Christian girl growing up in a war-torn Beirut[14] would not necessarily dream of a house on Rawcheh, that is, in the western[15], mainly Muslim part of the capital. She was rather hoping to be able to acquire one in

---

14. I saw (3):
I saw kids playing with paper pistols. They knew nothing about PlayStations or Nintendos or Walt Disney's enjoyable movies all saturated with pink and blue. They tore up blank pages out of their copybooks, and they folded them once, twice, three times to convert them into weapons. The children simulated the war that was whistling in their ears. The war was in wait for them like an ogre, to devour them once they grew-up. They dug trenches. They stood guard. They aimed. They shot. They fell. I saw children killing their childhood and their tomorrow with paper pistols. And the world was smiling stupidly.
15. 'Beirut el Gharbiyeh'.

Jounieh, or Maameltein, or Jbeil, or even Amchit, all largely Christian coastal cities.

It wasn't until she was 17 that the woman whose green eyes make trees stumble went to Rawcheh for the first time. Before that, it was just a picture on a postcard, or a vague place that her parents would talk about sometimes, when nostalgia hit them[16]. They would also talk about Cinema Capitol, Souq El Tawileh, and other mysterious places with abstract names that she could not relate to. She was a woman of the tangible, the tactile. And when her mom and dad strolled down remembrance lane, she used to feel like an alien. Her Beirut is not theirs. There was a gap, a clean cut. No connection, no build up. She might as well be from another country[17], with a totally different capital... *Thank God that memories, unlike genes, cannot be exported from one generation to another*, she thought cynically. The war had fortunately made her cynical. Cynical enough[18].

Her pragmatic friend Mireille – with whom she went, for 14 straight years, to Zahret el Ehsan Catholic School[19] – a school run by nuns who, like horses, saw life in black and white – used to laugh at her whenever they discussed their future plans and wishes, sitting at one of the white plastic tables in Abu Elie's Cafeteria: 'A house by the beach? What kind of a dream is that, you silly girl? You'll get all rusty from the humidity. Not to mention, you should strive to be "in the middle of the action", not in a lost isolated spot with the smell of fish for company. You are such a romantic[20].'

Now Mireille is a successful stock broker in New York[21],

16. Nostalgia: again, what a pain! Almost as annoying and unnecessary as gratitude or marriage.
17. If only!
18. Who said good things only happen to bad people?
19. Never do that to your children.
20. The woman whose green eyes make trees stumble is not romantic at all. (Or so she likes to think).
21. Apparently, she calls herself Myra now.

right *in the middle of the action*. She often closes her eyes in her big noisy Manhattan apartment, after a long hectic day on Wall Street, and dreams of having a house by the beach in Lebanon.

The woman whose green eyes make trees stumble took another look at the sea, closed the shades and went back to bed, waiting for Raffaele in the adjacent room[22] to come and wake her up with the usual cup of coffee and the kiss on the shoulder[23].

They had met on the 12th of July 2006[24]. She was having a drink[25] with her girlfriends in one of the pubs of Monot Street, El Pacifico. And there he was, gazing at her insistently with his piercing blue eyes via the mirror that faced the customers. He was with a group of friends, Italian tourists apparently. As soon as their eyes met he stood up and walked towards her. She appreciated this urgency. This getting-into-action *carpe diem* manner. She loathed those she called the 'slow-eaters', men who would just spend the whole evening glancing then shying away, staring at women back and forth, lacking the guts to leap into the fire. *None so blind as those who will not see*, she thought despicably. Those molluscs reminded her of a poem that describes exactly the way she felt, even though she couldn't quite remember who wrote it[26]: *When I*

22. Have I told you she couldn't stand sleeping with a man in the same bed?

23. They didn't really meet in 1975. They had actually met years after that.

24. The 2006 Lebanon War, known in Lebanon as the July War, was a 33-day military conflict in Lebanon and Northern Israel. The principal parties were Hezbollah paramilitary forces and the Israeli military. The conflict started on 12 July 2006, and continued until a United Nations-brokered ceasefire went into effect in the morning on 14 August 2006, though it formally ended on 8 September 2006 when Israel lifted its naval blockade of Lebanon. The conflict killed over a thousand people, widely reported to be mostly Lebanese civilians, severely damaged Lebanese civil infrastructure, and displaced approximately one million Lebanese. *(Wikipedia. org)*

25. Scotch. On the rocks. That was her drink. *Wine is for women*, she always says with a revolted frown.

26. 'Devil', by Joumana Haddad, from *Invitation to a Secret Feast*, Selected Poems, edited by Khaled Mattawa (Tupelo Press, 2008).

sit before you, stranger / I know how much time you'll need / to bury the distance between us. / You are at the peak of your intelligence / and I am at the peak of my banquet. / You are deliberating on how to begin flirting with me, / and I, / under the curtain of my seriousness, / am already done devouring you.

Over the 35 years of her life, she had had enough of men who let themselves be devoured, and needed a predator for a change. A real lion. And there he was, right before her eyes, indulging himself in the ceremony of the pre-banquet phase, just when the news of the first Israeli raid soaked the place with silence and stupor[27]...

The woman whose green eyes make trees stumble was now lying in her bed, immersed in a half-light which looked a lot like her, waiting restlessly for her 48 year-old lion's cup of coffee and shoulder kiss. That, along with the ritual of him gently taking her cotton socks off, was a morning routine she adored. And it astonished her, again and again, that she liked this habit so much, she who absolutely abhors customary practices and predictable, 'programmed' behaviors. *Could it be love?* She let herself slip towards that cliffy thought for a second. But she quickly swept the absurd idea away[28], and waited for him to appear.

And that was exactly what the poet/teacher/lion/sailor whose blue tears invented the Mediterranean Sea, did...

---

27. I saw (4):
I saw an old woman, her eyes closed, resting on a makeshift bed, in a school. Dead bodies in her mind, dead bodies in her heart, dead bodies on her chest, dead bodies on her right shoulder, dead bodies under her wrinkled eyelids. The old woman had her eyes closed, in order to be quicker in her journey into darkness. Her eyes were closed, in order to avoid seeing her soul hanging on the clothes line, drying slowly next to her grandchildren's clothes, yes, her grandchildren, those little devils who took her by surprise, and died before she did.

28. LAST WARNING:
This is the last time that I'm going to say this: What you are reading above is not a love story. It's a story about a woman and a man. Eventually there was no place for an old and dirty football in it, but this deficiency does not make a love story out of it nonetheless.

II. Never a Road Without a Turning (Mar 2005)

> *'There is an appointed time for everything. A time to give birth,*
> *and a time to die; A time to plant, and a time to uproot what is*
> *planted. A time to kill, and a time to heal; A time to be silent,*
> *and a time to speak. A time to love, and a time to hate; A time*
> *for war, and a time for peace"*
> King Solomon, The Bible, Ecclesiastes 3:1-8

He puts the key in the keyhole. Opens hastily. Slams the door.

The woman whose green eyes make trees stumble jumps, startled.

She jumps. Gets up. Quick. Quick. Mirror. Fixes her hair. Wets her lips (with her tongue). Quick. Quick. Gasps for a breath.

The man walks in.

He walks in. Doesn't say a word. Doesn't even glance at her. Sits on a chair. Grabs her arm. Pulls her brutally towards him. Sits her on his lap. Bites her lip[29].

The woman screams: 'Ouch..'

She screams: 'Ouch.' Scratches his back ferociously. Inhales the dizzying smell of his desire. Takes his cock inside her slowly, without any preliminaries[30]. Thinks: 'Sex is like a box of chocolates.' Thinks: 'Wow.' Thinks: 'Who would have imagined?' There she was, having her first real orgasm at 34.

Again: Who would have imagined? Certainly not her, after all those years feeding merely on cerebral stimuli, on what she likes to call her sexual electric chair, *the power of the virtual forbidden*[31].

He on the other hand, still had 'first times' to give. She liked that about him. In all her previous relationships, she never could prevent herself from hating the feeling that she

29. Her upper lip.
30. She is convinced that foreplay is a waste of time. A sheer waste of precious penetration time. And so *'seventies'*.
31. The forbidden, her head's clitoris.

was just the repetition of someone. Of something. At best, a premiere after a series of rehearsals. A sexual and sentimental déjà-vu. And (oh how) she hated being a déjà-vu. She wanted someone who would be able to say, after they did something, anything together: 'This is the first time I've ever done this. This is the first time I've ever felt like this.'

This, her 47 year old Italian lover was surprisingly able to provide. And much more[32].

They had met on the 14th of March 2005[33]. She was one of the demonstrators in Martyr's Square, downtown Beirut, and he was one of the journalists sent by *L'Unità* newspaper to cover the events of that historic day. She was screaming her lungs out with the crowd when she suddenly felt a gentle but firm hand from behind pick up her loose falling bra strap and put it back into place on her wild shoulder. That's when she looked back, and saw Raffaele for the first time...

How much does a heart weigh? She wondered more and more frequently these days. An 'empty' heart, without the extra load of love, pain, sorrow, passion, joy, disappointment, hope, affection, ache, excitement, desire, grief, regret, frustration, trust, doubt, anger, resentment, warmth, fear, ambition, faith, anxiety, suspicion, etc...?

And how can a heart relax when it gets tired? And is it, really, situated slightly to the left? Then how come she feels it everywhere sometimes, as if her whole body was nothing but

---

32. They didn't really meet on the 12th of July 2006. They had actually met one year or so earlier.

33. On 14 March 2005, Lebanon witnessed an unprecedented event: a demonstration of a million or more civilians protesting against the assassination of their former Prime Minister Rafiq al-Hariri a month earlier and demanding the withdrawal of Syrian troops from their country. The huge assembly brought together people from the country's disparate sectarian communities who until then had only ever joined in battle. And it engaged a whole new generation in civilian politics, when for so long the only way to get involved had been behind the barrel of a gun. The protests' impact was such that they completely eclipsed the gathering orchestrated by Hezbollah a few days earlier in an attempt to shore up the three pillars of Lebanon's then status quo: Syrian domination, the Lebanese security apparatus and the armed *Shi*'a resistance. *(Opendemocracy.net)*

a giant heart? Just like now, for instance, as she was thinking of him and of the bite on the upper lip he gave her this morning?

Could it be love? Was she becoming her worst nightmare: all mushy and sentimental? She lets herself slip towards that cliffy thought for a second. Then she remembers what her beloved grandma Jamileh, who committed suicide when she was seven, used to say, in order to console her on a sad day: 'Never a road without a turning, princess; never a road without a turning.'

So could it be love, then? She pondered on the idea some more, while she waited for him to appear.

And that was exactly what the poet/teacher/lion/ journalist/sailor whose blue tears invented the Mediterranean Sea, did NOT do.

That was exactly what the poet/teacher/lion/journalist/ sailor whose blue tears invented the Mediterranean Sea, had NOT done...

Yet[34].

34. CONFESSION:

They did not meet in Beirut on the 31st of January 1990. (They could have, but they didn't). Nor did they meet in Beirut on the 14th of March 2005. (They could have, but they didn't). Nor did they meet in Beirut on the 12th of July 2006. (They could have, but they didn't). Nor did they meet in Beirut on the 7th of May 2008. (They could have, but they didn't).

Didn't I tell you this was not a love story? It could have been one, if the coordinates of time and space had been right and opportune. It could have been one – *a great one, actually, one of those unforgettable legendary planetary ones* – if it weren't for one tiny fatal detail: The woman whose green eyes make trees stumble and the sailor whose blue tears invented the Mediterranean sea, just never really met. Two matching paths, two parallel souls that were definitely made for each other, that kept on coming nearer and further to one another, without ever crossing. Two perfect victims of quantum physics, of the continuum that somebody decided ruled our universe. One of so many vicious acts of spatial and temporal discrimination.

This is not a love story. After all, we can't pretend that something happened just because it could have, or should have happened.

No, this is definitely not a love story.

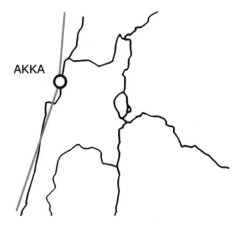

AKKA

The Passport

ALA HLEHEL

'Shalom, hello, can I speak to Shula please?'

'No one's working today. The Ministry of the Interior is closed.'

'Closed? Today's Tuesday.'

'*War*. Haven't you heard about the war?'

'But the war's in Lebanon and Krayot Shimona.'

'It's here too. Where do you live? Don't you know about the rockets that hit Krayot and Haifa yesterday?'

'What's Kraryot got to do with us? We're in Akka.'

'It's got a lot to do with us! All the government offices in the North are closed.'

'So who are you then? Didn't you say the offices were closed?'

'I'm the security officer. I guard the building.'

'But the building's shut.'

'It doesn't matter. It still can't be left unguarded.'

'And so what shall I do now?'

'About what?'

'About my passport. I've got to renew it – I'm going abroad.'

'You'll have to wait 'til the war's over. There's no one here to process your passport. Now if you don't mind...'

'But what will I do? When will the war be over?'

'Sir, please, no one knows when the war will be over.'

'A day, two days?'

'Come on now, sir, I'm telling you, I don't know. Good day to you.'

'The war can't go on for more than a week. That's what they said on the news. Didn't you hear? They were saying that none of Israel's wars with the Arabs have lasted more than a week.'

'No, I didn't. But it's probably true – we'll crush him like a cockroach!'

'Who?'

'Nasrallah[1].'

'How?'

'With planes and artillery. Can that terrorist hold out against our army for more than two days?'

'I don't know. Is that what you reckon?'

'Of course.'

'What's your name?'

'Vladimir.'

'So the war'll be over soon. They'll be back at work in the Ministry of the Interior tomorrow or the day after...'

'I don't know.'

'And what will I do if they don't come back to work, Vladi?'

'I don't know. Now good day to you!'

'Hang on! Hang on a minute please. Can I have Shula's mobile number?'

'What?'

'She knows me. She'll remember me. Tell her it's the writer who's going to Britain.'

'There's nothing I can do for you, Sir.'

'Give me her number then. She'll remember me personally. I was there a few days ago applying for a new passport. She and I talked about the tour I'm about to go on

---

1. Hassan Nasrallah – the current Secretary General of the Lebanese Islamist party and paramilitary organisation Hezbollah.

in Britain. She knows Britain really well.'

'I can't sir. It's against the rules.'

'Tell her I'm the man she recommended the 'Lonely Horse' pub in Edinburgh to, and she'll know who I am at once.'

'I can't sir. It'd be breaking the rules.'

'Aren't you allowed to ring her? You work together.'

'*I'm* allowed to, yes. But you're not.'

'Fine. You ring her then and tell her the situation, and give her my number.'

'Sir, please, leave me alone. I'm going to have to end this conversation now, if you don't mind.'

'But I'm in a state of emergency.'

'The whole country's in a state of emergency.'

'But my emergency's different to everyone else's emergency. This is a cultural emergency.'

'Excuse me sir, but I'm going to hang up. I only answered the phone in the first place by coincidence.'

'What do you mean "by coincidence"? Don't you usually answer it?'

'No. It's not one of my duties. But I thought you were my wife.'

'Your wife?'

'She's run away with the kids to her sister's in Natanya. I'm here by myself.'

'What are you doing here by yourself Vladi? Why didn't you go with your family?'

'Her sister doesn't like me at all. I gathered, from what my wife said, that it would be better if I stayed here.'

'That's extremely harsh. Leaving you here all alone...'

'I know. Her sister can go to hell!'

'Amen.'

'She hates me because I married her sister and not her.'

'So she's bitter.'

'What really hurt was realising, afterwards, that it's actually her sister who's the *real* bitch.'

'Her sister? You mean your wife?'

'Yeah. She left me here to get bombed on my own. I'm going back to Ukraine.'

'And my passport?'

'I'm going to hang up now. Good day to you.'

'No, no – hello? Hello? Vladi...Vladi!'

I went down the narrow alley that leads from Arafeh Square to the entrance of Akka's old city souq[2], and passed by the big fish stall. The fishmonger was standing at the stall, with a large dogfish in each of his muscly hands. He was being filmed on a video camera for an internet television channel, and he was shouting into the presenter's face:

'Know what I mean mate? I'm telling you, one time the net was dragging me along with it, see? I tied it up and used the crane – the winch – don't you know what a winch is?'

The confused young cameraman didn't know whether he was supposed to be answering the fishmonger's question or not, and frankly I didn't have time to stand and listen to the rest of the conversation. I carried on walking quickly through the souq, noticing that it seemed to be less crowded than it usually was. Then the air-raid siren sounded, reminding me once again: there's a war on.

A Katyusha[3] rocket? I found myself wondering. Then a voice came down from a balcony overlooking the street, and I raised my eyes towards its source.

'What's going on?'

'Sirens,' I snapped. What else could it be? Warning sirens meant war, meant bombs, meant air raids. Where was I going to hide?

'So d'you think Akka'll be hit, then?'

'Don't know.'

2. Souq - the permanent market quarter of any Arabic city.
3. Katyusha – a rocket, or a rocket launcher, built in and exported by Russia.

50

'No, Hassan Nasrallah wouldn't do it.'

'What, you think it's him who's loading the rockets and launching them?'

'So who is it then?'

'His soldiers, my friend, his soldiers.'

'I dunno mate, but it's him who gives the orders, isn't it?'

The sirens began to fade, then stopped completely. I didn't hear any near-by explosions.

'What did I tell you?' he said.

The war didn't seem to have reached the old part of Akka. Things were still being bought and sold in the souq, I thought to myself as I rushed along, and the Arabs there carried on coming and going, without their usual inner joy being diminished even momentarily. They walked with their own particular rhythm and talked with their own particular rhythm and shouted with their own particular rhythm; they cried, laughed, smoked, inhaled their shishas , ate, made jokes, laughed, grumbled to Allah, praised him, and then swore at him in the same sentence. They sat up late telling stories about the sea, argued over derision, argued over praise, argued over love, argued over hate, argued over their knowledge of the old city and its stories, and they could spin an equally good yarn by embellishing a true story or an imagined one. They ran behind the darkest shadow and they ran after the rising sun, they slept a little while by the sea and they slept a little while before dawn – all of this to their own special rhythm. It was as if the salty sea breeze had created a private world inside the walls of the old city of Akka, incomprehensible to outsiders, who would never have been able to fathom its symbols, or crack its highly complex code. Perhaps that was why the rhythm of this ancient city protected it from the war, and from its tense atmosphere. Perhaps that was why, on the fourth day of the war, the souq was somehow not in the same realm as the Katyusha rockets.

But what about my passport? Just before I reached the

third alleyway inside the souq, I saw the door of the house. It was an ancient house, from the time of the Crusades, like many of those in the old city and the city wall. It had a low door, behind which lived the Judge, who was of course not a judge, but a clerk in the Ministry of the Interior in Akka. He wasn't even a clerk in the full sense of the word, but more of a clerical assistant – making coffee, cleaning the offices, and singing the state's praises on payday. The Judge, as people in town called him, was my surefire inside contact for getting my expired passport renewed and being able to set off on my reading tour. I would travel all over Britain: our former guardian, and the founder of the Jewish state, may Allah grant them both long life.

The door was closed. I stood there and knocked at it with all my might; when I got tired of knocking, I turned towards a perfume and spice shop tucked away behind a large vegetable stall. As I approached the shop I saw Hawker filling a bag with his special fish spice mix. He was the originator of this exact recipe, never divulging the secret of its make-up to anyone, no matter who they were. This combination of fish spices of which he was the master had made him the most famous spice merchant in Akka, to the point that when people wanted to eat fresh fish they would always ask, 'Is it with Hawker's spices?'

Hawker was tying a knot in a plastic bag he had just filled with these red, invigoratingly scented fish spices. He took fifteen sheqels from the young girl he was serving, then accepted another two coins, pressed them to his forehead, and held them up as high as he could reach, saying, 'Allah recompense you, dear – send my regards to your father.' Then, to me, 'Hi, when did you get here?'

'Just now.'

'Well come and sit down, and let's catch up.'

'It'll have to be another time...'

'Go on, have a seat,' as he pulled out a small wicker chair, 'you know they've locked Picasso up?'

'Locked him up?'

'Of course – you know they arrested him yesterday, don't you? They chucked him in the cells.'

'Why?'

'What do you mean, why? What do you think he was selling, bro, za'atar[4]?'

'Oh, poor old Picasso... so is he out yet, or what?'

'Of course he's not, who'd get him out? His decrepit mother? None of his uncles or his friends'll bail him out anymore – don't you think they've got enough fucking problems of their own to deal with?'

'What about his wife?'

'Ha, his *wife*? Expecting help from her'd be like dancing in total darkness, and hoping to attract an audience of passers-by... His *wife!* Honestly...'

'So he's still in the detention centre then?'

'Why are you so bothered about him? They'll let him out in a couple of days. They know nothing they can do'll change *him* – his criminal record's longer than the old city wall.'

'Whatever you say... But I really pity Picasso. He just can't handle being locked up, you know?'

'Well you can go and bail him out then, can't you? Go for it, bail him out if you're so upset about it... Just have some tea and chill the fuck out.'

'OK, OK, I am. Anyway, where's the Judge?'

'At the Ministry. Where else could he be?'

'The Ministry's closed. "There's a war on, sir."'

'Whatever, let them shut it then, we're better off without it.'

'No we're not, I want to go abroad and my passport's expired.'

'Where to, insha'Allah[5]?'

---

4. Za'atar – a savoury mixture of thyme, sesame seeds and other spices which is eaten all over the Levant. Also used as a slang term for marijuana in Palestine.
5. Insha'Allah – God willing. Said automatically, often in a secular way.

'Britain.'

'Is something wrong?'

'A literary tour.'

'Much money in it?'

'A bit.'

'It'll be easy, insh'Allah. The Judge'll be here soon, there's nowhere else for him to go.'

The siren let off a piercing scream, and I jumped up in terror.

'Calm down mate...'

'I hate that shrieking!'

'Get a grip on yourself, come on.'

'But, Hawker, really, I mean it's all so *frightening*!'

'Oh, come on, it'll be alright, you'll see.'

The siren gradually faded away, eventually stopping completely.

'See, I told you so...'

I found the Judge sitting in Tony's restaurant, eating hot chickpeas with tahini, lemon, and garlic. I pulled up a chair and ordered chickpeas with fava beans. The congregation was streaming out of the entrance to the Jazar Mosque, sharing customary blessings for the end of prayer-time: 'May Allah hear them, may Allah answer them.'

'So Judge, where've you been hiding?'

'There's no work, so I thought I'd fix the boat up. See if we can get a bit of a decent catch in.'

'So have you mended it?'

'Not yet. There's no rush, is there? It sounds like this is a right bitch of a war, two month's worth, three even. That's what they said on Al-Jazeera.'

'Don't say that, for God's sake! Are you some sort of military analyst now, or what?'

'That's what it looks like, I'm telling you. His Eminence made a speech yesterday, and we're up shit creek, basically.'

'I want my passport. I'm going away.'

'You haven't got a hope in hell, my friend... No passport, no Ministry - all the Jews are in Eilat.'

'And Shula?'

'Shula? What about her?'

'She's got my passport, hasn't she? I left it with her a few days ago. In her office I mean. So it could be renewed. And I need to get it from her, but the Ministry's shut, and Vladimir–'

'Vladimir?'

'He says there's no one there and that they'll be back when the war's over.'

'He's right, yeah.'

'What do you mean, *he's right*? What can we do about my passport?'

'Nothing. Everything'll be sorted out when the war's over.'

'I'm telling you I've got a literary tour in Britain and you're telling me to wait 'til the war's over?'

'Well what do you want me to do about it?'

'Come with me and we'll get my passport.'

'Where from?'

'What do you mean where from? From the Ministry!'

'The Ministry! The *Ministry*, he says... Just dip your bread in your ful...'

'So what, that's that?'

'You want me to break into the Ministry of the Interior?'

'You wouldn't be *breaking in,* at all – you work there, don't you?'

'Well, yes...'

'We'll go there, knock at Vladimir's door, and get the passport before he goes back to Ukraine.'

'Ukraine?'

'We won't even have to–'

'What's this about Ukraine? Is Vladimir leaving?'

'Mate, his wife left him here and went to Netanya. The bloke's so pissed off he's talking about it to anyone who'll listen.'

'This is million dollar news, my friend! Eat up, go on, tuck in – your ful's on me!'

'Why are you so excited? What's going on?'

'If Vladimir's off I'll be taking his place. I'll be on at least a thousand sheqels more – have a can of 7-Up bro!'

'Congratulations, that's great... So, if you could–'

'I'll need a gun, if I'm a security guard.'

'Great, that's all we need, you starting us a new front in the war!'

'Do you reckon they'll give me a gun?'

'Aargh, of course they won't! Give an Arab a gun? You'd have to be a collaborating dog to get a gun.'

'Can't we get someone to pull some strings for you? Doesn't your dad's cousin work for them?'

'Leave my dad's cousin right out of this. So are you sure Vladimir's going back to Ukraine?'

'Of course he is. He's been here four years and nothing's ever worked out for him, it's been shit from the start. He was a mechanical engineer over there, and over here he's a security guard. What's keeping him in *this* fucking dump? Is his grandfather buried here or something?'

'Give us a falafel.'

'That's a good idea. Hey Tony, give us a cola mate, a diet one... got a fag?'

'Come on then, come with me.'

'Where to? Have some tea.'

'I've had some.'

'Some coffee.'

'Come on mate, are you up for doing me this favour or what? What's the matter with you?'

'Go on then, give me my orders.'

'Come with me to the Ministry. You work there and Vladi knows you.'

'Vladi! You've even got a pet name for him...'

'What've you got to lose?'

'Alright then. But lunch is on you.'

'With great pleasure, my friend.'

'Prawns?'

'Prawns.'

'Done. Meet me at the Ministry in two hours.'

'Why not now?'

'Now? As if! What about the boat?'

'So you're suddenly going out to sea now, are you?'

'We have to live, mate... Allah curse the hour.'

'What hour?'

'The hour we were created in.'

'Exactly.'

'By the way there bro, isn't Britain near London?'

I was heading for my flat when my mobile rang. It showed my family's home number, in the village. *Oh God, not now...* But I knew from experience that if I didn't answer, my mother would call the border control, the coast guard, the hospitals and the morgues.

'Hello?'

'Well love, when are you leaving?'

'I don't even know if I am.'

'Why's that then, son? Won't the Jews let you? Let's talk to your dad's cousin, seeing as he works for them.'

'No mum, the Ministry's closed, my passport's expired, I'm meant to be leaving in two days, and Shula's disappeared. And don't even mention my dad's cousin, that arsehole!'

'Who's Shula?'

'A clerk at the Ministry.'

'Isn't there anybody else?'

'I'm tired, Mum, really tired... I didn't sleep well.'

'Are there rockets going off over there?'

'Not really. Loads of sirens though. What about there?'

'Are you joking? The Israelis've got their rocket-launchers right beside us, at the border, so Hezbollah are firing at them with Katyushas, and we're stuck in the middle, getting fucked!'

'Keep calm Mum, it's alright. How are you all doing?'

'We're fine. I've made you some za'atar to take with you.'

'*Za'atar*? Are we still living in 1948 here mum, or what?'

'For the relations. On your dad's side.'

'Dad's relations? That's a new one.'

'You know that one of your dad's cousins on his mum's side's a refugee in Wahdat refugee camp in Jordan?'

'Really?'

'And her husband's from Irbid.'

'Uh-huh?'

'Well her husband's cousin on his dad's side is married to a man from the Gulf.'

'Uh-huh?'

'And that Gulfie owns a big export company.'

'Uh-huh?'

'Which your dad's cousin on his mum's side's son works in.'

'In London?'

'No, in Abu Zabi.'

'Abu Dhabi.'

'Yeah, whatever it's called.'

'So where does London come into it?'

'Well, his wife's family are in Ain al-Helweh refugee camp in Lebanon.'

'Uh-huh?'

'And one of her brothers works for UNWRA[6].'

---

6. UNWRA – United Nations Relief and Works Agency for Palestine Refugees in the Near East.

'Uh-huh?'

'He's married to a Palestinian woman from Sweden.'

'Uh-huh?'

'And her family were originally from Miron, near us.'

'Uh-huh?'

'Well everyone from Miron was displaced by the occupation, weren't they love?'

'I know mum, I know.'

'And the rest of her family are in Belgium. They're our kin.'

'And what's that got to do with me?'

'What do you mean love? You're going to London and you're not going to visit your dad's relations and take them a nice bit of Palestinian za'atar?'

'What makes them our relations, mum?'

'They're our inlaws.'

'So you really think I'm going to take za'atar with me to London so I can give it to the wife of one of the relations of my dad's cousin on his mum's side's son's wife?'

'What's wrong with that love? You can take them some fatier[7], too.'

'You what? Take za'atar and fatier to London?'

'No love, to Belgium. They're in Belgium.'

'But I'm going to London mum!'

'You can get from London to Belgium in the time it takes to smoke a fag, love.'

'Bye Mum. I've got to go to the Ministry.'

'Didn't you say it was shut?'

'I'm going to open it Mum! I'm going to open it!'

'Off you go then son, and God protect you. Don't forget to wear clean pants though love, ready for the airport security.

And don't talk about politics in Britain. Your grandad, may he rest in peace, was a freedom fighter back in the days of the

---

7. Fatier – a delicate savoury pastry usually stuffed with spinach or cheese.

British mandate, resisting the invasion...'

Quake always spends the day sitting by Bizani harbour, smoking peacefully. He watches the sea, and pays no attention to anyone. Up above the place where he sits there's a new modern-looking café, and behind him, to the right, a long-established and old-fashioned restaurant, right on the waterfront. He's absolutely convinced of the inevitablity of a huge earthquake coming and destroying everything: if not this month, or this year, then definitely next month, or next year.

His location is a strategic choice – it's taken him a long time to work out, with the utmost precision, that it will be the best of all possible places to be in when the earthquake strikes. His justification for this consists of the following: the earthquake that's on its way will be a deadly one, measuring more than seven on the Richter scale. It will be long and violent – an expected duration of between forty and sixty seconds. Over seventy percent of the houses within the walls of Akka's old city, and over thirty percent of those out in the new city, will collapse and bury their inhabitants alive. It would, therefore, represent the height of all foolishness to spend time in, or to sleep in, a house in the old city. The only thing that would even come close to a folly as astonishing as that, would be to choose somewhere far from the sea as your place of ongoing, and preemptive, refuge. Nowhere on dry land will be safe, even out in the open, because not only will the force and duration of the earthquake destroy the city's houses, but it will crack open the actual streets and lanes and alleyways too – and you can believe me when I say that Quake doesn't know which would be worse: to die beneath the rubble of your house, or for the ground to open up like a mouth and swallow you, without mercy.

Taking perennial refuge at the sea shore, on the other hand, is the most logical solution, because no matter how violently an earthquake rocks the land, it can't crack open the sea like it can crack open the earth. Quake is always stressing the absolute implausability of our cousins' stories about Moses parting the sea with his staff, even though they appear in the Bible and the Quran. He says the Jews managed to sneak that story into the holy books, so as to plant an image of themselves in the collective imagination as omnipotent beings who part seas and perform miracles; but there has never been any chance of the all-knowing Quake being taken in by this hoax, and so he awaits the earthquake with tranquility and confidence. He takes no notice of people mocking him, or of their scorn of him for sitting, day and night, at the sea shore. And if it wasn't for his skill at catching fish with his long hook, and selling his catch every day, he would never have been able to support himself. He would have died, cold and hungry, long before he ever had the chance to fulfill his dream of escaping, alone and unscathed, from the devastating earthquake that is on its way.

It was obvious that Quake was not in the mood to talk to me right then. We weren't close friends, but we sustained a kind of wary collusion that we would communicate, mainly, through silence. I don't remember ever talking to him about anything other than the earthquake, and his projections about it. I'd learnt to read his mood from the way he sat: if he was squatting, with the fishing-rod between his legs, it meant he was open to company and conversation. If he was sitting, leaning back on the sea wall right up against the Mediterranean's waves, with the fishing-rod propped-up expertly against a big rock, it meant he would be closed to any attempt at conversation or communication.

That was how I found him, as I made my way home from Tony's restaurant. I sat down beside him without greeting him, as he wouldn't have answered me in any case. I was contemplating the sea when I saw him suddenly grab the fishing-rod and start to pull on the line, now firmly, now tenderly, until he raised it out of the water and there, hanging from the end of the line, was a big fish. He grasped the fish with a small towel that had been covering a wicker basket at his side, and unhooked its jaw; then he threw it on to the pile of fish in the basket, and covered the basket with the little towel. He scooped up a little fried dough,   fixed it onto the hook, cast the line back into the water, and lent back once again.

Quake had found his freedom, I said to myself, and he wanted to preserve it at all costs; that was why he was waiting for the earthquake to come and wipe everyone else out but spare him, leaving him to his own devices. As I got up to leave, smiling to myself at the brilliance of this insight, he grabbed my hand and held out a big fish wrapped in a sheet of newspaper. I took it, and he smiled at me, then went back to keeping watch over the sea. Carrying the fish, I set off towards the little harbour.

'Where are you going?'

'Home. I've got some fish with me.'

'There's a demo on.'

'Where?'

'At the main road. Out of town.'

'Against who?'

'Against the war. Against Israel.'

'When?'

'Now – come on.'

'No, I can't. Later.'

'What do you mean later? I'm telling you the demo's *right now*.'

'Well, you know, the war'll be on for ages – I'll march another day.'

'Another day'll be no use. Public action needs to start right away. The government needs to be told that this is an illegal and disgusting war, and that they're destroying Lebanon. I mean, hasn't anyone ever been kidknapped here apart from their soldiers? What about the thousands of Palestinians in

Israeli jails? And the Lebanese prisoners? Don't you give a fuck about them?'

'Hey, come on, I know all that. But I've got to find a way of getting hold of a passport.'

'Why? What's happened to your passport?'

'It's expired, and I'm leaving for Britain.'

'For Britain? With the situation like it is?'

'What's the situation got to do with it? There aren't any Katyushas in Britain.'

'There's a war on, matey, a war! Haven't you noticed?'

'So what do you want me to do about it? D'you think I can catch the Katyushas before they land or something?'

'You're being defeatist. It's not like you...'

'Well, fine, leave me alone and may Allah be pleased with you. Bye.'

'So you're not coming then.'

'Nope.'

'Fine, suit yourself. Hope London does you good.'

'Right.'

She went one way and I went the other. I hadn't got more than a few paces away from her before my conscience began troubling me. *Go on the demo! Go on the demo! It's the least you can do! Go on the demo! Make some noise, be heard! Go on the demo! For God's sake!*

I turned and hurried towards her, caught up with her and fell into step beside her. She ignored me. She obviously didn't want to talk to me. I volunteered, 'Have you all been writing slogans for the march?'

'Nasrallah Nasrallah, our habib[8], strike, strike Tel Aviv...'

'They could jail you for that one.'

'Don't come then, if you're scared.'

'Of course I'm not scared, not at all...'

Just before we reached the little crowd that had gathered

8. Habib – beloved, darling, companion, mate, hero – a very versatile and emblematic term of endearment, admiration and respect in Arabic.

near the central station, at the edge of Akka's new city, I remembered that I was carrying a bag of fish. The July sun was blazing down and my whole body was pouring with sweat, soaking the armpits of my shirt and making a wet stain in the middle of my back – so what would become of the fish?

'United we stand, from Gaza to Beirut!
Alive alive alive, from Gaza to Beirut!
United we stand, from Gaza to Beirut!
Alive alive alive, from Gaza to Beirut!'

'Nasrallah Nasrallah, our habib,
strike, strike Tel Aviv!
Nasrallah Nasrallah our habib,
strike, strike Tel Aviv!'

'A national salute, to the mighty proud Beirut!
A national salute, to the mighty proud Beirut!'

'South South hang on tight,
there's no fear and there's no flight!
South South hang on tight,
there's no fear and there's no flight!'

'We're saying it loud and we're saying it clear,
We don't want no Zionists here!
We're saying it loud and we're saying it clear,
We don't want no Zionists here!'

'King Abdullah you're a wimp,
King Abdullah, America's your pimp!'

My mobile rang suddenly. I moved away slightly from the little crowd.
'Hello?'
'Where're you?'

'Here. Where're you?'

'At the Ministry. D'you forget, or what?'

'No, I didn't forget. There's a demo going on...'

'Well then, it's up to you – your passport or the demo?'

'I'm on my way! I'll be there in a minute.'

I extricated myself calmly from the crowd. Luckily for me, a car full of Jews stopped beside the demonstration at that very moment. A young man in the prime of life got out and began shouting in Hebrew at the small band of marchers:

'Wait 'til we've finished with Nasrallah – then we're coming to get *you*. Then you'll have something to shout about. Filthy Arabs! Go to Syria!'

By the time he said the word Syria, I'd already crossed Bin 'Ami Street and begun hurrying towards the Ministry of the Interior.

'Am I late?'

'Let's go for it. Before Vladimir leaves.'

'Haven't you got a key?'

'Ever seen an Arab with a key to the Ministry?'

'Right then, let's go.'

Vladimir was sitting on a chair outside the door of the Ministry of the Interior, with his ear glued to a little transistor radio, his body facing some railings overlooking a big shopping centre, and his back to the door. He didn't notice us. He was engrossed in listening to what was, as far as I could hear from this distance, classical music. The Judge made a signal to me and I followed him, walking cautiously, just like he was. Quietly, we entered the Ministry offices. They were still and silent, and all the lights were off.

I knew where Shula's office was, so I went straight towards it. I opened the door with the utmost delicacy, slipped through it, and tiptoed across the room. I opened the drawer I'd seen her put my passport in when I was there, on the right hand side of the desk. The drawer was full of thick bundles of passports, held together with big rubber bands. I sat down at the desk and opened the first bundle, and began to work my way through them, opening each one at the picture page, to identify its owner. I got to the end of the first bundle and still hadn't found my passport.

'Got it?'

'Not yet.'

'Hurry up, before Vladimir sees us. He's a right bullet-monger.'

I opened the second bundle, then the third. Nothing. There was only one bundle left. As I picked it up I heard a stifled shout from the Judge:

'He's coming! He's coming!'

I stuffed the bundle inside my shirt and moved it around to my back, so that Vladimir wouldn't notice it bulging out of my belly. I stood next to the Judge, gripped by fear. Our eyes followed him as he came into the big public waiting room, and crossed it, coming towards the side Shula's office was on. I swallowed, and whispered to the Judge:

'Look, why don't you talk to him? You work here, don't you?'

'Not exactly.'

'What do you mean "not exactly"?'

'Up 'til a week ago.'

'Did they fire you?'

'For being an Arab.'

'For being an Arab? Why though?'

'There were a few problems...'

'Problems... You mean we're in the middle an office, inside the Ministry of the Interior, and you don't actually work here?'

'Kind of, yeah.'

'So you're after Vladimir's job because you haven't actually got one at all...'

'As soon as he goes past the door we'll make a run for it.'

Vladimir was nearly at the door to Shula's office, but he didn't stop, and he didn't look in our direction even once. He was still carrying the little radio, holding it to his ear. He passed right beside us, and went on down the corridor. I understood from the way the Judge moved his head that we needed to get moving. I followed him cautiously. He leaned over a little and looked out into the corridor. He signalled to me with his hand, so I followed him. He stepped out of Shula's office, and crept off towards the main entrance. I leaned out of the door, as he had, and looked towards Vladimir. He was slowly walking away from me, at the end of the corridor, the radio to his ear. I stepped through the door, heading for the main entrance. The Judge had disappeared, so I guessed he'd made it out of the building. Suddenly I heard a shout in Hebrew:

'You!'

I spun round to face Vladimir. How stupid! Now he'd seen my face. I should have fled, straight away, without looking back. And now here I was, standing in front of him, begging for mercy. I was transfixed for a while; but it didn't take him long to get his gun out of its holster, and it didn't take me long to get my legs moving and throw myself into a frantic and hysterical sprint.

I didn't look back again, even for a moment: all I could think of was what the Judge had said about Vladimir being so trigger happy. I had no intention of taking a bullet from Vladimir the Ukrainian, protector of our passports.

I pounded away without stopping for a second. I had never known I was such a good runner, considering my weight, how much I smoked, and how long it was since I'd done any sport.

When I came alongside the intersection where the demonstrators were all still standing and chanting their slogans, I decided to stop for a while. I got my breath back, dried my sweat with my shirt, put the bundle of passports down my pants, and joined the marchers. I wanted to see if anyone was

67

pursuing me.

'Where were you?'

'Here. A bit...'

'Did you run away from the Jews?'

'You could put it that way.'

She walked away from me in disdain. Where was the fish? For God's sake, I'd left it on Shula's desk. What did that mean? Would it be useful to the police, as evidence? I didn't think it would. A fish in Akka? What kind of a lead was that? Fish was like currency in Akka. They had nothing on me. *I must calm down*, I told myself, *alright? Calm down. And have a shower. Come on, better go home.*

'Lebanon our love, we're like hand and glove!
  Lebanon our love, we're like hand and glove!'

'Martyrs rest after your fight,
we'll carry on your struggle day and night!
Martyrs rest after your fight,
we'll carry on your struggle day and night!'

'Traitors and defectors, prepare to eat lead!
Traitors and defectors, prepare to eat lead!'

I lay on the little mattress I'd chucked on my bedroom floor. The July heat was unbearable in Akka, especially with the humidity of the sea air; it clung to one's body, turning it into a sodden mass of sweat and odours, impossible to neutralise with any deodorant, no matter what the adverts promised about their great effectiveness. I'd just bought a new kind two days ago, a famous international brand, which comes in an elegant and enticing black roll-on dispenser. The black dispenser is made particularly elegant and enticing in the advert, when a fashion model – who is undoubtedly gay in real life – raises his arm to apply it to his armpit. Overcome with desire at the sight of this, his lover, who is also a model, throws herself onto his smooth and hairless chest.

A stubborn drop of sweat was running down from my armpit towards my back, making its slow and disgusting path. I felt the droplet send a shudder through my body – partly as a reaction to something creeping along on my skin, and partly with the realisation that I'd begun to sweat, less than half an hour after getting out of the shower. I decided to lie on my side, so that I would squash the foul droplet before it reached my back.

I looked at the television screen. The Channel Two correspondent for police affairs was talking to the news reader. I reached for the remote control, which was lying amongst the passports strewn over the bed. I turned the volume up as I started contemplating, in pure bliss, the official Ministry of the Interior stamp which adorned my passport, as well as the Hebrew phrase: 'extended expiration date 31 July 2010.' Little by little, it dawned on me what was being discussed in the news studio on the screen:

'... Police still don't know if the theft of a number of passports from the Ministry of the Interior's offices in Akka is connected to the latest events in the current war, and to a potential attempt to use Israeli passports in enemy operations against the state. In any case, the Ministry of the Interior and the border police have cancelled the twenty passports stolen today, which will therefore not be valid for travel, even if the pictures in them have been changed... I interrupt this story as I'm just being informed that air-raid sirens are sounding at this moment in and around Haifa and Akka.'

I froze, stunned: then I heard the terrifying scream of the sirens fill the air.

I jumped up from the bed and stood in the middle of the room. As usual when I'm at home in the summertime, I wasn't wearing anything except my embroidered boxer-shorts. I didn't know what to do. The air-raid siren? The passport? I thought about it for a second: the passport?

Without knowing what I was doing, I found myself opening the door onto the balcony, stepping out onto it, and standing looking down into the street. It was full of little Arab children running around like hysterically happy demons, shouting like lunatics, 'Katyusha! Katyusha!'

Translated from the Arabic by Alice Guthrie

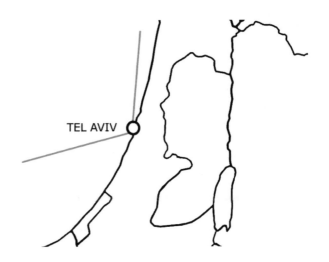

TEL AVIV

Meningitis

Yitzhak Laor

Night has descended on the military headquarters. Darkness veiling the barracks like a dewy tarpaulin. A man's shadow stretches from the top floor of the Ministry of Defense's office like a large bird, then vanishes, leaving Yair alone in its calm decampment. 'Like a killer round the corner,' Psoriasis had said, while putting on his full pack in the dark. Yair knew how to hide his feelings. He would have given a lot for these moments to last for he loved his new army buddies, his comrades from all corners of the country, with all sorts of medical conditions. Among them was even an epileptic guy, as well as three asthmatics, four with ulcers, and two suffering from depression. All had been enlisted for one reason or another, and guarded, for one reason or another, the state's most sensitive compound – not counting the US Embassy, which was guarded by Marine soldiers. Yair enjoyed sitting with them in their rooms, while they got ready for the night watch. He could have even forgiven his father, who forced this enlistment on him, because perhaps this was what his father had had in mind, that he would go out a while into the world and make new friends. After all you can't be caged up at home like a nocturnal reptile not even knowing the names of the kids in class (he knew, he knew, he knew very well, he only told his father that he didn't know), and besides, he will never forgive his father. For now, the joy flooding through him has

73

nothing to do with his enmity towards that shadow falling from the window, that transient fear like an invisible gust of wind, not fear, but a clear knowledge that he is doomed, and that he must not fear, for nothing will alter the verdict. Not murder, nor madness, nor suicide. Dad sits and watches over him here as well. He is here because of Dad, and Dad is here because of him. And no, not suicide. He would never commit suicide, he is of sensitive skin, and his life is not worth the drama.

He loved his friends from the unit, particularly because they made fun of themselves, called themselves by the names of their medical conditions - even though he was the only man in the platoon who was known by his real name, that is the one given to him by his parents. He too had wanted, hardly dared, but had almost asked to be known by his, but something prevented them from doing so. How very much he longed to be nicknamed like them with contemptuous names, but then his father did not allow him to mock himself, did not sanction this kind of humour, believed that with this kind of humour his son would never get well, that this kind of humour was too Jewish, not Israeli enough. So supposed Yair, for he had never told his father a thing of his friends' customs and certainly didn't dare confess that here too he was an alien, an outsider, and yet, on the other hand, here he loved them, a great love he loved them, and was capable of standing up and hugging everyone.

During the day, when they would see an officer marching their way, even if they were walking in a group, they would immediately disperse, and switch to walking in a long line, so that each of them could salute the same officer separately, and keep him saluted in earnest for a long time, with a muscular arm, and back stretched, for, as it's written in the General Staff Order, an officer must return a salute to every saluting soldier. They did so because they were individualists *par excellence*, and yet also cultivated a platoon's pride, a culture of collective memory, in addition to a sense of humour. They called themselves 'The Swiss Guard, with no colours.' Psoriasis was the cadet on duty, and his roommate's name was Gastritis. In the neighbouring room lived Bronchitis, and with him also lived Psychosis and Sclerosis. Those who knew nothing about diseases thought that the group in question was a bunch of modern Greek poetry aficionados, and those who knew nothing about modern Greek poetry, thought it had something to do with classical Greek poetry - classical Greek poetry being a heritage that belonged to us all, although Hitler too prided himself on it.

Today is the anniversary of Bronstein's death and in front of the guard barracks flickers a memorial candle. The soldiers are sitting out in the open by the picture, and saying things about him, some things they had already heard and some completely new. They are stern. In the 'commemoration corner' of the Guard Room hangs an enlarged photograph of Bronstein, who was nicknamed 'Meningitis'. Below the photograph flickers a memorial candle. Above the photograph inscribed in big letters are the dates of his birth and death; at hardly twenty years of age Bronstein-Meningitis had died in the line of service, from Meningitis officially (and in truth from suicide by hanging, after he found out that he was originally not enlisted because he wasn't Jewish). The commemoration corner for Private Bronstein was vigorously cared for, only during free time of course, and their own commander, Sergeant Nisim – no official disease, but in secrecy they called him 'Borderline' – was extremely proud of the red geranium garden and the nasturtium flowers which, according to him, he nurtured almost single-handedly. Beneath the photograph also lay a large book of commemoration. Once in a while the guards wrote in it in memory of Bronstein, and even urged officers passing through – some of whom were of considerable importance, their contribution to the state's security invaluable, some even having won the Israel Security Award, or reached such grave heights as the Israel Prize for Literature, or for Social Work, only more confidential – to sign,

LIVERPOOL JOHN MOORES UNIVERSITY
LEARNING SERVICES

as a sort of a yearly petition in memory of Bronstein. Many senior officers had written words of praise to the obstinate soldier.

Major General Zalman Zal – whose ass was kissed every two weeks in his own office by Israel's writers and poets – signed as well, before dashing off to watch the new video for the 'Ezekiel 4' tank, which he had only just developed, much to the dismay of those who questioned the next armoured war. 'Parachuting is dispensable too,' ruled Major General Zalman, 'and yet you don't abdicate parachuting, so what's it to you if more and more tanks are getting built? Yes, more and more and more.' And since Zalman Zal did not know how to operate the VCR, and never learned, at his disposal stood one of the soldiers. Not Yair, of course. He did not want to go up there, and his friends understood – it not being so bad having to scrounge cookies with cheap chocolate filling, and see all the important people from the bureau telling each other military secrets. Besides, the soldier on duty's task was simply to freeze, using the remote control, the picture on the screen at precisely the moment when 'Ezekiel's' belly rose up over a deep-water obstacle.

Night after night Major General Zal would watch the video, as well as during lunch breaks. Every viewing he'd roar with pleasure, 'Now, now,' just as the tank stopped, rose, and revealed its undercarriage like the belly of a giant crocodile, hungry for prey after a long winter, or however those writers who kissed Zalman's ass described it, because Zal had studied Philosophy just as they had. Each year a new movie about 'Ezekiel' came out. From what's been said up till now, it should be understood that Israel's writers also sat and watched the tank lifting its belly like the white marble horses of Piazza Venezia. And as mentioned, the task of pressing pause and serving cookies to the writers and painters was always given to one of the soldiers. When Zal screamed: 'Where's the dork?' the soldier, who'd be waiting in the hall behind the door, would immediately come in, and say: 'Here, Sir!'

'Who's here? What's here?'

'The dork's here, Sir.'

When Yair's father came to visit, Zalman Zal remembers… a gentle man, very complex, at nights he invented tanks, and in the mornings urged his office manager, Lieutenant Vered, to recite for his friends lines from the greatest poet ever to rise to military commission, Nathan Alterman. And Vered would indeed recite: 'And the land will grow still / crimson skies dimming, misting / slowly paling again / over smoking frontiers,' and sometimes she'd get the rhymes wrong intentionally (Vered Tsela may have been a big coward, but she loved to provoke danger, danger to be honest aroused her, and instead of 'dimming' she'd sometimes say 'brimming', or 'slimming', but it made no difference, because what mattered was the rhyme and the meter)… Well, only when Yair's father came for a visit, did Major General Zal remember not to joke like that, because Yair too served under the Chief of Staff Guard, which was the highest up he was allowed, and that too only with Dad's intervention with the Major General and the Major General's intervention with another Major General and the intervention of that other Major General with a Colonel and downwards to Sergeant Borderline. Yair's limited service pained his father. Not that he would have liked to see his son fall in the line of duty. On the other hand, most fighters didn't fall in the line of duty and why must one always think the worst?

Evening. Yair sat on a prickly mattress covered by a wool blanket (emitting an odour of flee repellent and damp wool), watching the others as they got ready for their watch. In the neighbouring room someone had forgot to put on his long johns, and everyone burst out laughing at how he's have to take everything off again in the dark, the full pack too, only to put on his long johns. Without complaint, they would agree to leave the lights off each night, before going out to their watch, making all their preparations in the dark, even checking the magazines, and Yair loved them for this sacrifice, for him. He was loved in turn, not only because he had brought so much candy from his leave (his father had wanted so very much for him to have friends, and so had, himself, baked abundant cookies and even bought a large quantity of chocolates). It's possible that Yair's friends noticed his efforts to endear himself to them, gently, without imposing himself. He would laugh at the drop of a hat. Any talk of theirs provoked his laughter, as if he had never come across unserious people, and now any unserious expression seemed hilarious. He himself did not know how to be funny. Yair was extremely handsome, and any laughter would make his eyes well up like a child awoken from sleep. And if they went into a huddle, he did not squeeze in to listen, nor was he hurt, but assumed it of matters beyond his capacity. Perhaps he did not dare to be angry at them since he was in their debt. After all, it was because of him that they were constantly being watched from up there.

Bewilderment would spread across Yair's face every time he was asked too blunt a question. He never raised his voice. Sometimes he would picture himself with his head tattered, or hung, or both, veins slashed. Ah yes, why did they do it all in the dark? Because of the father's observations from the window above.

After a four hour patrol around the fences, they would approach parked vehicles and peep, by command, into them; later they'd return to wake the next shift, take off their uniforms, put on civilian clothes, and through their connections in the next shift, would go out, without permission, from the base, into the city whose electric rashes were as colourful as eczema. They would sit together in a bar – Yair would not come with them, afraid to run into his father with some woman, literature or film lecturer – speaking quietly, like a national minority, mocking themselves in earshot of the waitress. That's how they would pass their nights and their days, patrolling, sleeping, taking walks in the city and sleeping again and again patrolling.

Yair did not partake in guard duty. He was exempt, a red

written note which said he was prohibited from guarding, because of the night and the fog and the smog. Instead his duties included a weekly roll-call and a talk with the commander. Were his friends hurt by the fact that he did not guard? Not in the least. (Again, for this, he loved them). In their platoon they had plenty of guard soldiers, after all so many parents tried to enlist their sickly sons, and each of them got here thanks to some connection. Perhaps they were not angry with him because he was such a beautiful boy, pale and soft spoken. His gentleness he got thanks to his two older sisters who spoiled him – Yair had grown up without a mother, a son to his father's old age.

The father's heart would sink, almost give in to his son's refusal to enlist, when he heard the boy's screams at night. 'I am not Erlking,' he said to himself in horror, not knowing if his own dream was provoking those screams, or the child's, and yet, at breakfast, from within the stillness, the boy's plea fell on deaf ears, because the father knew he was doing this for his son's sake, or at least he told himself as much, and told his son, and the two girls who wouldn't dare argue, and Zalman Zal, yes, he said so too to Major General Zalman Zal. One can sympathize with the father. All his life he had wanted to escort a son to the Enlistment Office, and later escort him to the Absorption and Classification Base. All his life he had wanted to attend the Basic Training graduation ceremony, and had wanted to attend the section commander's course graduation, and the officer's training course graduation. Very gradually, when the child's health did not improve, the father let go of these dreams. But of an unglamorous military service, a grey service, he did not let go, could not have let go.

At first he would say these things to Yair with a smile, as if the son's declaration of not going to the army was a sort of joke. Of course it had nothing to do with the fact that the father was a national figure. All fathers are national figures, perhaps the other way around, all national figures are fathers, never mind. For he never said a word to him of the nation and its needs, because in any case Yair did not demand of him what the nation needs, paratrooper officers, for instance, rather it was all about, son – he called him son, his sad smile did not waver, he had a sad smile, the father, and his son hated that sad, photogenic smile – it's all about, son, the duty bestowed upon you to overcome your ailments and to be like everyone else, after all one day I will not be in the world, and who will take care of you then? The son wanted to say: 'When you aren't in the world, I'll take care of myself just fine,' but checked himself (was terrified of his father; his father will never know this, because fathers are doomed not to know): 'Arabs also don't go to the army.' His father nodded in comprehension and did not reply. He had a deep comprehension of his son's need to rebel against him. He did not comprehend anything that was not from within himself, as the son's father, and comprehended the son only as the father's son.

When Yair had persisted in his refusal to enlist, the father took him to Major General Zal's office for a conclusive discussion. It was a difficult moment for the father. Up until that day Zalman Zal knew just a small portion of the father's agony over the son. After all, the father had never spoken of the son, always just of the girls. The Major General knew of the older daughter's marriage and of the other's doctorate, but even of them they had spoken very little and preferred to engage in nominating laureates for the Israel Prize, the Hebrew Literature, Science of Judaism, Social Work and of course the prestigious National Security Award. Yair, on his part, was not aware that the beautiful walk through the city, and along its beaches, would end in an office overlooking the guard barracks, in which he would be serving in two months time. It was truly a fun day. Dad had never had so much time for him. They went to the movies, later sat in a café, and even though many people approached Dad, Dad was not nice to them at all and insisted on sitting with Yair alone. Later they went to clothes stores, shopped for fragrant oranges at the market, and went to the port. They even tried to sneak onto one of the boats anchoring there, and in short, Yair tried to get his dad to do things that the dad was embarrassed to do, and dad went everywhere Yair led him to, because he was a good father. They stopped by a fishing boat, which had brought up in its net many revolting octopi, and since octopi are not only revolting, but unkosher, they had no buyers. Except for Yair who wanted an octopus. His father bought him one, under the condition that he would not ask him to carry the small bag after fifteen minutes, as had happened with the dog they bought him: Dad had to take him out every night so that he would poop outside and not in the living room, in front of the guests. So, Yair promised and picked the biggest octopus, and off the two walked down the streets, the son carrying a huge octopus in a small plastic bag, the father walking a little ahead, perhaps out of embarrassment, even though the town's dogs were chasing both of them. A fight between two of the dogs shortly broke out – guessing that soon Yair would throw the octopus, and only one of them would win it – and went on and on; they almost bit one another. And people trailed behind the dogs. Maybe they were the dog owners, maybe they were passers-by who thought this was some sort of street theatre, Holbein or something. A few of the *danse macabre* participants knew the father, and followed him being dragged by his son holding a stinky octopus and ten dogs, two biting each other, through the city streets, and since Yair had now thrown the octopus to the dogs, the fight between the two big ones stopped, because a small dog, carrying away the small bag in his mouth, had escaped. Dad said something about Manfred Herbst, whose legs had carried him without him knowing where to. 'Do you know who Manfred Herbst is?'

'You've already told me this so many times and in relation to practically any subject… Is there any other book you know?'

Yair was tired and suspected his father of trying to improve his physical fitness. And it was as if by chance that they arrived at Major General Zalman Zal's office. At the gate they

81

let the father through without checking his documents, he was a regular bore there and the soldiers did not read anything of his whatsoever; what did they care? Zal was sitting, of course, in front of his VCR. As they arrived he was calling Vered, asking her to turn it off, and return the cassette to the video library, where all had been marked 'Ezekiel 1', 'Ezekiel 2', 'Ezekiel 3', etc.

The father didn't know how to begin the meeting; after all they had gotten there by chance, as it were, perhaps embarrassed by the thought that the octopus odour had stuck to them. Zal did not stall, saying that he himself had ordered his granddaughter to enlist in the army, despite her being mad, as everyone knew, mad as a hatter, a drug addict and even more so a man-addict (worse than drugs, believe me, I know men), and that to be on the safe side he had ordered Vered to help his granddaughter in all sorts of matters which she could not manage herself, like renewing her driver's licence, or managing her bank account, or paying her electric bill, because here we are all one big family. Yair too, of course, would be a part of this family, and Zalman Zal launched into stories of his clerks' devotion, especially Vered Tsela's, whom he loved like his own granddaughters, which is why she recited rhymes and meters for him, and she of course saw her service here as a great honour. Major General Zalman Zal, let's be perfectly clear, did not screw any of his clerks. On the contrary. He took care that they would not be harassed by all kinds of males, and took care to make sure the girls kept secret all kinds of love affairs they had, with all kinds of officers, because crazy is the girl who'll pass up the opportunity to fuck a little in the army, and here everyone is one family, said the Major General. Indeed all the clerks ranking all the way up to Lieutenant-Colonel had to listen to every phone conversation the Major General had, on the amplifier, and on the extensions – a part of their culture being an expansion of the Major General. On this rested their pride, or pleasure, or both.

Yair's father had thought that his old and admired friend would have a few more convincing arguments, but all Zal's explications came down to the importance of serving in the army, for the people and for the son of the people. For the people, why? Because the people need an army. For the son of the people, why? Because the son of the people must be a soldier for at least some time during his life, if not throughout his life. Well, Yair already knew all these arguments, and yet, Major General Zalman Zal was not finished. For a long time now he'd suspected the instant coffee here gave him gas, therefore he farted. He had no problem with farting. He who sits in a tank all his life, learns not to be shy. All you need to do is lift one side of your behind and let it out. Yair was stunned. He searched for his father's eyes, but Dad pretended, as if he too farted whenever the need arose, and perhaps he did fart. At home – he didn't.

'You probably believe that the paratroopers are the force of the future. Am I right?'

The Major General spoke in a loud voice, looking over at Lieutenant Vered Tsela, whose eyes washed over beautiful Yair in jet streams of light. Ah, how Vered loved boys like Yair. Yair too. And the Major General, with the bitterness of a veteran of the Armoured Corps, spoke, and the son looked at his father, and the father was flooded with admiration for the Major General, or perhaps was flooded with bewilderment, in any case, his dismal and famous smile did not leave his face. 'Nonsense, nonsense,' cried the Major General, and waited for Vered to reiterate – she was an outstanding memoriser, but that said, as much as she was taller than Yair, and even older, she could not take her eyes off of him.

'Nonsense, the next war will be an armour vs. armour war. Anyone can see that. Tanks will pound along the deserts from here to Kuwait, and our soldiers of the Armoured Corps will charge like Formula One drivers, especially in the new tank, 'Ezekiel 4'. Watch the screen. Where's the dork?'

The smile did not leave the father's face, like a Chinese

diplomat, and the dork came in, froze the screen, grabbed a cookie and left quietly, so all watched the rising tank, like a giant turtle, threatening never to land. 'Ezekiel 4', or '3' froze.

'Why would you volunteer for the Parachute Corps? For the parachuting? This parachuting business doesn't impress me. I refused to take a parachuting course. I just didn't want to. Not afraid, no. Because of the hassle. You see?'

Yair nodded. Zal went on, as befits a military leader, noting the slow penetration of his forces into the boy's mind: 'What do they do in those famous commando units of theirs? Sit and wait and wait and wait. What are they waiting for? For the day when they will be able to attack missile bases in Caucasus' mountains?' Now he turned to the father, who was trying to say something, but Zal continued: 'And in the meantime, I ask, in the meantime what do they do? In the meantime they kill people up close, with knives, or guns, in Tunisia, in Beirut. And to keep an entire army for this? Just because one day there will be a commando war?'

When they left – Vered had not dare say a word to them – Yair told himself that everything, this entire wonderful day, was just to get him to this talk with the commander. He'd been deceived all day. His great love for his father had swallowed a fruit, and in it a large pit, bitter, asphyxiating, stinging. He hated his father. They did not speak all the way home. In the cab he was suffocated by the desire to cry. The father was offended. It is unclear to us why, but every so often the father would get offended and would not talk about it – a nightmare for his kids – for hours, and all that they could do was guess what had offended Dad. Go deal with *your* father's childhood memories!

Later the son surrendered. What had he gone through, from his desire to cry in the cab to this surrender? A great deal. But in the end, he'd been promised that he would serve down there, beneath the office, and ever since his father had come every day to spy on him from the high window. Every once in a while the father would walk over to the window, and the Major General would say to him: 'Sit, sit, he'll see you watching him. It's not good. Let him be a man already.' And the father, his eyes shrinking involuntarily, as if carefully selecting his words, would say without turning around: 'He doesn't know I am here.' The father knew of course that the son knew. After all the son had asked him during one of his leaves: 'Why do you even go there so often? To spy on me?' Yair had wanted to say so much more, wanted to say every night, wanted, since that walk in the city, to say something that swelled and swelled, and turned into something violent, contemptuous, offensive, like 'I wish you had loved Mom the way you love this fat Major General, I wish you had loved us like you love him, I wish you had loved me like you love yourself, but you are not even in love with him for being him, you are in love with him because he is a Major General, and when you find another Major General, woosh, you will ride off to the other Major General. Why do you love Major Generals so much? You probably want me to become a Major General, that's why I'm so sick, because you've always wanted me to become a Major General.' He did not say all this balderdash, but once he dreamt that his father was pissing through him, holding him like in an open-jawed stone fountain, and urinating through his mouth. Sometimes he thought of hanging himself in the guard barracks, in the light, so that his father would see him from up there convulsing, and would rush down to save him, but would be too late, and would only manage to get him down from the ceiling, a corpse. One day Dad will lose it, one day I will wipe that constipated smile off of his face.

Well, today, as mentioned, is the anniversary of Bronstein's death, may he rest in peace. Everyone respects this anniversary, and as of last year, thanks to the petition, it has become a General Staff event, meaning an event of this base, ours. After a prolonged explanatory effort, he is now mentioned, in the basic daily order, which Sergeant Borderline pins up on the cork boards, while two guard soldiers stand to attention by the candle. A soldier on duty asks the passers-by to lay a flower, or put down a few words in the commemoration book for the soldier who fought such a long battle just so the army would enlist him, in spite of his poor health. And here comes a Major General, Moti the moron. Conversing loudly, because that's how he talks, with a girl soldier, an admirer, who also talks in a big voice so that everyone can hear her talking with Moti the moron. Yesterday her father reprimanded her, when she told him how careful she was not to be alone in a room with Major General Moti. He was extremely insulted by this remark, her father. 'I don't like your delusions. I never liked your delusions. For as long as I remember you, everyone hits on you. One day you will say the same about me. It's the fashion now, isn't it? But Moti is a Major General in the IDF. You can behave like a human being and refrain from making dirty insinuations.'

And since the guard soldiers had been preaching all day to the passers-by in their barracks to act appropriately, one of them now steps up to Moti as well. To the Major General's credit, let it be said, he apologises right away, attempts to stretch his sloppy shirt, stands at attention for a moment, and suddenly salutes, sticking out his chest and forcefully stretching his palm to his temple. The soldier with him, being very moved by Moti's invitation to escort him again to his office, she too salutes, and a button, exactly between her two squished breasts under a pointy bra, snaps. Gastritis, for his part, wants Major General Moti to end his salute, and approaches him cautiously, saluting, taking two measured steps backwards, standing to attention, saluting again – there is probably some kind of order, thinks Major General Moti but he is not familiar with the procedure. It does not cross his mind that he is being mocked here, who would conceive of it? – Later Gastritis says quietly: 'Major General, your honour, asking permission to speak.'

'Make it short, I'm busy.'

'Major General, I'll make it short: we need help.'

The Major General hates requests for help, but Gastritis tells him that the guard is trying hard to establish an award on behalf of the army in their friend's name, Bronstein, may he rest in peace. The Major General is impatient, although the soldier with him waits. He has already envisioned her in his mind's eye pacing back and forth in his room, naked, with only the black army shoes and white socks on her feet. 'Who is this Bronstein?'

'I'll make it short. He wasn't enlisted on account of health problems, insisted on enlisting, and ran a public campaign. His parents turned to the army authorities, and participated in the public campaign for his enlistment, along with his high school friends. The press were also involved in the campaign. We have a bellicose press, like any democracy, and ardent editorial articles spoke of the struggle against this refusal to enter the Israeli army, which should begin with the positive, not the negative. In the end the army surrendered and despite the sensitivity he had been inflicted with as a child, he served in the guard platoon. He died in his uniform, while guarding. Recently we turned to the Base Commander asking him to establish an award for the sick soldier for distinctive service in Bronstein's name. Our appeals have been to no avail.'

'But why should someone who could have evaded the army and didn't take advantage of that be given an award?'

'Because otherwise life is not the same.'

The Major General looks into the soldier's sad eyes, and promises to help.

Everything might have gone as planned with the committed soldiers, if it weren't for the fact that the Major General tended to forget the promises he made, and perhaps his soldier's naked parade made him forget this one. Luckily for us it was so. In that respect, a Major General's flawed memory is a source of hope for the entire nation. May there be many

87

such forgetful leaders and commanders. And anyway, it would have been a great embarrassment to us all, if the truth about Bronstein's life and death were to come out. He did not have a memorial day, because he did not die, because he was not born, because there never was any Bronstein. Because he was the heart of our platoon's service: we made him up in order to sanctify him and to mock the entire world through him.

When Yair was let in on this comical secret, that was of no interest to anyone, and gave us a strange satisfaction, he'd been explicitly asked not to reveal the secret to his father. He was not offended by the request. On the contrary. He felt very proud to have been given a chance to betray Dad. The idea of betraying Dad, and with this beautiful story of a soldier that never existed to boot, excited him, and he volunteered to tell the life story of the deceased. Yair wrote beautifully. If it wasn't for his father, he would have really accomplished something through this, but his father did not like his writing, was afraid that he would only be praised because he is his son. 'Bronstein's Memoirs' by Yair was the most touching chapter in the book, because it was written out of rage. No one could believe that the boy made the story up. We will never know what is real with people that do not hesitate to use their tongue.

Evening descended. Lights rose from the guard barracks. The father walked over to the window, but Yair was no longer there. He'd tricked his father again, taken off under the protection of the darkness, and instead of feeling gratification, felt a great sadness, once again seeing himself hung, his veins slashed, as he walked towards the gate. At times he thought of going on watch with his friends, but feared his father would take it as his triumph.

Outside the gate a Major General, Moti the moron, picked him up in his car, and asked: 'Where are you headed, soldier?' Yair shrugged and said in his typical impudence in places we have yet to encounter him: 'Are you checking if I have a pass, or what?' The Major General said: 'No, no, I'm just

driving to the north of town and thought you wanted a ride.'
Yair went with him, and suddenly, just as he was about to get
out, not far from the beach, he said: 'Tell me something, this
army really doesn't bore you?' The Major looked at him and
said: 'You know what? Now that you ask, I think so, yes. But
they need us, don't they?' Yair said: 'No, I don't think so.' The
Major thought a moment, then assumed Yair was joking. Yair
looked at the grand night and the lights, and imagined seeing
a huge bird flying and taking up with her the entire city.

Translated from the Hebrew by Yael Manor

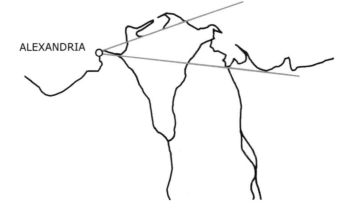

Midnight on the Outside

GAMAL AL-GHITANI

Telephone Message
From: Department of Industry   To: Department of Health
    Re. your message to ourselves, dated today, concerning the availability of an empty bed in the rest-house, on your part; we request the reservation of a place in the name of Mr. Youssef Abdel-Rahman, newly appointed employee, on our part.

Relayer of Message
Signature

*

The houses gradually recede, the small shops, the advertisements, the glass signs; a man calls out at a passing collective taxi; a song drifts from a nearby house, one they always play at this time, one o'clock in the afternoon; movement on the street builds up. This is when the people in his distant city return home from work. As soon as he saw his father he would shout: 'Hooray! Daddy's here! Daddy's here!' It is not simply that the song reminds him of days gone by, but it stirs up the dust of buried sorrow inside him. Sweet, bright, radiant days when he ran on the sands of the beach, when his eyes encompassed the sea, when Samia was in his arms. She fed him the white grilled fish with her hand, wiping drops of salty seawater from his lips. Now he bites his lip. The turning of the carriage wheels is monotonous, the air around him chill. They told him this town was very cold, especially at night. His mother advised him: 'If you feel cold, put an old newspaper over your chest.' Perhaps she is standing on the balcony now, knowing that Youssef will not appear at the bend in the street. His father will not have arrived yet, but his sister might be home by now. He used to go from room to room, pinching his sister, asking her if anyone had bothered her. He would eat quickly, reaching out to chuck his mother on the chin, as she told him what she had seen when she went down to buy the fish: how she looked everywhere until she found the fish he liked – there was nothing in the shops but small perch; how on her way back she met Mrs. Amina, who told her about Mohamed, who had come to get engaged to her daughter Suad, who has never been to school and has three sisters, so Mrs. Amina would take the first decent young man that came along for the girls. Youssef would listen. Then he would ask his mother if no sweet, attractive girl had come to ask after him, and she would raise her hands in supplication to Almighty God to speed that day when she would see her son's bride. The carriage passes the last of the houses, the uninhabited area spreads out, the palms become denser, the horse trots on.

*

Wednesday, 22 December

Were the doctors afraid of infection, preferring to be isolated? To reach the town I have to walk half an hour along a dusty road completely devoid of houses or huts. When I first saw the building it was exactly as I'd imagined it: very large rectangular windows, shut and looking like they were never opened; the balcony ringing the whole of the second floor, supported by wooden posts planted firmly in the ground. At the time it reminded me of the houses of my distant city, with their wooden façades – oh, the smell of the washing hung out in the salt sea air! If I close and open my eyes I see the clean streets and shops, the beautiful women, the sea. Not a day passed that I didn't see the sea. At night I was terrified of it; if I was walking I was afraid of finding myself in its waters, so I walked far from the wall in case a rough-fingered hand reached out to pull me into the depths. I kept away from the swash of the waves, from the palpable unseen deep. The building looked ruined. As I crossed the patchy rest-house garden I was convinced somebody was watching me, and my back shuddered. I climbed the external staircase, the wooden steps covered in dry leaves. The silence was like the desert hills, as though the world had been destroyed. My virginal, wide-eyed city no longer existed, even though I had left it just hours before. Suddenly Abdel-Maqsoud appeared. I was tired, my eyes almost closing with sadness and exhaustion. He is tall, with a long neck; his face is hard, always looking straight ahead. He didn't welcome me. It was the same coldness I had been met with by the people in the office. I heard nobody say they were glad for my safe arrival. I exchanged glances of dislike with them, especially the smartly dressed youth and the old man with the voice full of spume. I followed 'Uncle' Abdel-Maqsoud, a painful throbbing in my chest. I couldn't believe I was so far from Samia, from the sea. I rested my bag in front of me, then let my head fall forwards for a while, my eyes closed.

Youssef

*

1. Dr. Galal Mahmoud Mursi, 12/7/68 to 13/7/68.
2. Mohamed Fawzi Abdel-Salam, 20/8/68 to 21/8/68.
3. Youssef Abdel-Rahman, 11/12/68 to...

*

'So there's no one but me in the rest-house, Uncle Abdel-Maqsoud?'

'That's right.'

'If I went into town now and came back late, who'd

open up for me?'

'Me. You'll always find me downstairs. I hardly ever go into town.'

'But it's a terrible road, Uncle Abdel-Maqsoud...'

'Look, Mr. Youssef. This area's always been uninhabited. Nobody comes near it. The road's dangerous, and there's plenty of bad people around.'

'So it's not safe to come back at night?'

'Well, if you're brave enough to do it, Mr. Youssef...'

★

Wednesday, 22 December

I don't know what would happen to me if I hadn't brought my exercise book and pen. In my city I don't write at all for months at a time, but today I've resorted to it twice. In the mid-afternoon I broke my regular habit and didn't sleep. The cold is bitter, so I can only read under the blanket. And if I went into town, who would I spend the evening with? The cafés are few and small. In my own town if I sit at a café in another neighbourhood they give me suspicious looks – so what would it be like here, where everybody knows each other? My father told me that the people of this place are like secluded women: they finish their work and go home, not leaving the house again until the following morning. He said: 'God keep you from the bad people.' I replied, my eyes tearing, as the first station bell struck: 'I'll spend my time studying English and reading books.' He advised me to try to find another young man my age, an outsider also, and rent a room or a flat together. I know why my father said that: so that no one could fool me into getting involved with a girl who might take me away from him and cut off what money I might be sending home to the family. Anyway, none of the women of this town are as beautiful as the girls of my city. Oh, for the crowds and the lovely sun on a Friday morning at the main tram station, as the wind blows full of the blue of the sea! It was at the station that I first saw Samia, wearing a white blouse, orange skirt, black stockings, and large white shoes. Her eyes were... what colour?... honey. I saw her like a light rain that falls gently on a hot day, like small petals covering a pavement in the last days of March — like a pale, distant star, with wide eyes, a trim nose, strawberry lips. I knew I would never see her like again. If I had been born a girl I would have wished to be just that way. For a while I tried to form relationships with girls who lived in our street, but I was hesitant and I trembled before I could speak to them, though my friends encouraged me to be bold. Now there she was, and something in me that I could neither see nor understand told me if I lost her, I would spend the rest of my life away from all women. I went up to her and told her my heart quaked when I saw her, and I felt we had been friends for a long time. She stopped, looked at me with a smile on her face that I could not fathom, and said: 'Oh, and what else?' An odd persistence took me over. I asked her name, and what year she was in. First year secondary, she told me. She went on to say that I was charming and good-hearted. But suddenly she stopped, and asked me to go away. I told her my name was Youssef, that I had an intermediate commercial diploma, that I would soon begin work, and that I planned to take the general secondary exams, because I needed to go to university. I said we could study English together. She laughed and said again that I was very good-hearted. I asked her if she meant this as a compliment or an insult. She then asked me politely not to walk any farther, as we were near her aunt's house. I told her I would wait for her and walk back with her, even if I spent the whole night there. She smiled and said there was no need. I followed her until she disappeared, and made a mental note of the address of the school. Suddenly I yelled at the top of my voice and set off running, gulping in the sea air, swallowing up the yielding asphalt of the road. I wanted to stop everyone I saw and tell them what had happened, I laughed, I joked so much with my mother that she thought I had been drinking, and I told her she was the greatest mother in the world. When I met her the night before I went away there were tears in her eyes. I said I might be away from her for months. She said she would go with me. I squeezed her hand. The cafeteria was empty apart from us, the coloured lamps lit up intermittently, water from the rain lay in the lower part of the garden, the sound of singing came from far away. I kissed her, and ran my fingers through her hair that was as soft as night. She swore on the grave of her mother to send me a letter every three days, telling me everything that had happened to her, to the city, at school, whether it had rained, if the sea was rough. If she went to the cinema with her father and stepmother she would tell me exactly what films she had seen. When we left the cafeteria the air tasted of carnations. The light of the high lamps was constricted, like her voice as we said goodbye. If she were here with me, everything would be different. I went back to listening to the drone of silence. I looked up at the very high ceiling as I asked Abdel-Maqsoud about this marble fireplace. He said the English used to warm themselves in front of its fire. I asked him if he had been here at the time of the English. He told me it was they who had built the rest-house for the irrigation engineer, and that he himself had been one of those to carry the stones and beams of the building on his shoulders, after which he was given a job here. He stopped, and seemed unwilling to talk further; he put down the jug he was holding and left. I don't know what he's doing right now. He seems not to have gone to sleep but to be watching me through a hole in the door. My blood shivered, but I've shaken off the thoughts that were pushing their way into my head. I pondered the books in an attempt to pick a novel to kill the rest of the time with.

Youssef

★

His hand grips the edge of the window. The ribbon of bright light flashes by, revealing the carriages that look like a single long block, rushing over the joints in the rails: the twelve o'clock train, from the Cataract to Cairo, first class, non-stop. In his mind, Youssef follows the men sleeping on the blue seats of the carriages; others are drinking tea and eating cakes in the dining car. They appear bored – it is a long trip. If Youssef could ride the train – in a matter of hours he would be in Cairo, then another train would take him to the sea. How long, and slow, this time seems that he will spend here before he can take a holiday and go away. The light flows softly outside, and the faint lights of the distant town make it seem farther away. He suddenly notices some men on the stone bridge – is Abdel-Maqsoud among them? He cannot make out their faces. Their long arms seem to touch the water of the canal. He dare not close his eyes; the slightest movement might alert them to his presence. From far away come mysterious noises of which he can only make out what sounds like gunfire. Is that connected with the business of the men? He does not know where they came from; they appeared suddenly; perhaps they came out of the rest-house? At once everything he sees is gone, the soft light evaporates, the features of the room are lost, below him and above him is blackness. Has he been struck blind? Is he surrounded by strangers? Dwarves? Giants? The sun will not rise on them. He is doomed, he will not live the moment after this one. No one will know. Abdel-Maqsoud will not protect him. He struggles half-paralysed towards the bed, his fingers tighten on the blanket, which he wrenches roughly and wraps around his body. He stubs his toes against the sharp-edged chair. If they cut out his tongue right now he would feel no pain. He leans his back against the door. He is totally alone, a pip thrown into space empty even of stars, of the earth, of grains of sand, of Samia, of the scales of the palms.

★

'Good morning... No, I honestly didn't hear anything... You see, the lights go off after twelve... The town generator stops.'

★

Thursday, 23 December

The director called me in, asked me what marks I had achieved in my diploma, and my typing speed. He gave me three letters and asked me to copy them. His hair was shiny and his teeth white; he spoke gently. Every now and then he picked up his long pen, which was immersed in a brass inkpot, to mark a single word with it. I nearly told him that the rest-house was uncomfortable and that I would not be going back there tonight, but I hesitated: what were my excuses? As I left his office I was surprised to find my colleagues waiting for me. They asked me what Sir had said. I said: 'Nothing.' They were silent, and regarded me with animosity. My young boss came over and gave me ten disbursement forms to review. He looked at the many files in front of me and told me not to mind if I had a lot of work, but this was a necessary part of my training. I said it was all right. Then he asked me what the director had said. I said: 'Nothing.' And I really didn't see that he had said anything worth repeating, but he stood up straight and looked at me with undiluted hostility. I was exhausted, I felt as though my eyes were full of stinging soap, and I was nauseous. The image of Samia pierced my heart. After a while he came back and pointed to my small bag. I told him what was in it: my exercise book, a novel I hadn't finished, three envelopes, and my wallet, because I didn't carry my money in my pocket. For the others to hear, he said this was no place for reading novels, work was to be taken seriously, and he personally didn't like any employee under him to bring novels in during official working hours. At two o'clock, as I was signing against my name, the old office messenger came to ask me to see the director. I turned round and, without paying any attention to the looks they gave me, went into Sir's office. He smiled, and I noted with surprise that he was quite short, which he had not appeared while sitting down. He said he hoped the work was not too much for me. I relaxed, and no longer felt the need for sleep. It was like the moment when I saw Samia coming from the direction of the sea. I said: 'Not at all. The work isn't tiring.' I promised myself that I would talk to him in a minute about the rest-house. I almost said I felt I was talking to a fellow human being for the first time since I arrived. He said: 'Do you know any of the employees here?' I said I didn't. He was silent for a moment, then said: 'I'm like you in this place, but while it may not matter to you as a single man, I have a family living here. Unfortunately, these workers never stop talking about me.' He paused, then went on: 'Of course, this is bothersome.' But if he knew exactly what they were saying the matter would cease to hold such importance. All I had to do was listen to what they said and report it to him word for word, without any embellishments or omissions. 'By the way, have they said anything to do with me today?' I said I couldn't remember. He waved his hand and appeared unconcerned, but asked me to pay attention from now on. I went out, and the desire to sleep returned. I walked to the bus station and sat on the passengers' platform. Three schoolgirls stood some distance from me, waiting for the small diesel bus that connected the town with the nearby villages. I didn't look at them. What did they have, compared to Samia? And where was the sea? Where were the shiny roads thirsty for the rain? The distant sails like the wings of that hunchbacked bird? Where was the joy of those two pots of pure honey? She is laughing, beating me to the tram: we get off at the end of the line and walk beside the sea, which breathes deeply in and out. We start to run, and sit down at the end of the stone jetty, me resting my head on her thigh, or wrapping her in my arms. Somebody might see us, but I pick strawberries and pears and drink the juice of apricots. Once her sighs subside, she talks of the hopes we pray will come true. Travel has to be the first thing. We couldn't conceivably live our lives in this city, Samia. When we're married we'll go to Sudan, to Eritrea, to Beirut, to Europe, we'll explore distant cities together, we'll sit at cafés at the foot of mountains. We take out a pen and a piece of paper and we write down the costs of our first journey. Obstacles arise, but we overcome them. Ha! Perhaps Samia's thinking now about what we said? Do any of those office workers know what detailed plans we drew up together? Is the director aware of our dreams? Their world seems to stop at knowing what *they* said, what *he* said. It enters my mind to get on the first train to my city, to Samia, to lay my head on her breast and cry, to weep without tears. I stood up holding my small bag. The platform was empty of passengers, the girls had gone to their far-off villages, and Samia had now left school for the day.

Youssef

*

'Remember what I spoke to you about before, Uncle Abdel-Maqsoud? How about sleeping in the room with me? I'll give you a shilling a night. Two beds: one for me, one for you. Every night a shilling. Go on, please: it's just that it's a big room, and the house is empty, and whole area's kind of scary.'

*

If he had a radio, he would listen to voices from all over the world: This is Beirut, This is London, Iraqi Republic Broadcasting from Baghdad, The Arabic Broadcasting Station from Moscow, Aden, Algiers. The voices would mix together, becoming indistinct. A keen yearning moved through his blood, to listen to a song close by. The voices of the men would start up soon on the bridge. It was two hours since Abdel-Maqsoud had come in and looked all around him, his eyes examining everything in the room as though this was the first time he had been there: his clothes hanging on the rack, his bag that was still open, his shoes, his socks, his red-and-black striped towel, his comb. He asked him what he was doing with all these books, but he remained silent. Then he asked him how old he was. Youssef said: 'Nineteen.' He said he was young. Then he lay down, wrapped up in the blanket, and that was the sudden end of their conversation. Youssef did not know what to do now. Should he turn off the light, or read by it? Abdel-Maqsoud had not asked for it to be turned off. He did not know if they had returned to the bridge; but perhaps Abdel-Maqsoud would know who they were. Then he would think Youssef was watching them, and might do something to hurt him. Youssef bit his lip. Despite the appearance that he was fast asleep, a hidden sense told Youssef that Abdel-Maqsoud had not slept and that if he could see his eyes from the other side he would find them open. The light dimmed; it would soon go out: the last cinema showings had just emptied. He had been to the cinema four times with Samia; she had told her stepmother that she was going to study with a girl from her class. His eyes roamed about the ceiling as he wondered what Samia was doing now.

★

Saturday, 25 December

Abdel-Maqsoud scared me this evening. He spent a whole hour staring at me, still as a rock. He stopped me asking him what I wanted to – about his life, the people who stayed at the rest-house, his solitude. And in the air a smell of sweat rose up that I had not smelled on him before. Even though he stretched out an hour ago, turning his face to the wall, he's observing me now: his ears hear my movements and count the beats of my heart. I'm tired. Samia's letters haven't reached me yet – every day I ask the postmaster in the south of the town. I'm upset and close to crying. I don't know why Abdel-Maqsoud is so mysterious; I don't know why he's like this.

Youssef

★

It is approximately two in the morning now, the night's
shadows at their deepest. Youssef has not slept; even the twelve
o'clock train has not passed. The bed creaks suddenly. He
holds his breath. The rustle of a gallabiya. Abdel-Maqsoud has
not gone back to lie on his bed. What is he planning? Does
his silence and the absence of any movement hide something?
Is he going down to join the men on the bridge? He is not
heading for the door, he is approaching him. The moments of
nightmare: his scream trapped in his nose, his body paralyzed,
his father's call: 'Wake up! Wake up!' If only. Who would rush
to him here? Who would shake his body to wake him up?
The bed creaks; it is not a nightmare. Abdel-Maqsoud's sweat
fills his nostrils – Abdel-Maqsoud feels his body – his thick,
rough hand caps his mouth – his hot, sticky breath creates a
shudder behind his ears – the weight of his body – the other
hand reaching to his pyjama trousers – the room drowns in a
viscid oil. If he could call out... But who would answer if he
screamed?

★

You used to say that when you looked at my face you felt a
sadness that did not pierce your heart but filled your soul with
something of which you had no knowledge, and I asked you
how you could be sad when you looked at my face. You said
you were baffled. Here, every evening around sunset I go to
study with my friend Suad, and I see your face more than
once on the way: at bends in the streets, in front of fruit juice
stands. I remember our plans for travel, and I imagine myself
having gone away on my own, to a small town at the edge of
the world, with paved streets and an old church. I sit at a
restaurant with a wooden terrace and suddenly I see you
crossing the road. I wasn't expecting to see you, so I jump up
from my seat, and I call to you. You're astonished: who could

be calling to you in Arabic in this place? You open your arms, you spin round. I ask you what brought you here, and you ask what brought me. Joy can't contain us. You wish we could be turned into two small birds who would fly to the tops of mountains covered in snow. Ah! Do you remember when I was going down the long, iron, red-carpeted staircase of the cinema in front of you, you said: 'Now you're descending the steps of the Boeing.' And when we went out onto the street we said we had passed through customs and we had nothing to declare. Then you described everything you saw...

Youssef: In a single day I think of you for two days. Remember the prawns? That long road spread with shadows? Sometimes I think the city has become a ruin without you. I have known the cruelty of parting only when my mother died and when you left. I'll write to you every three days, maybe every two, maybe every day. And when you write to me, don't write less than four pages of foolscap – I must know everything about you, major and minor: what you eat, how you sleep, what you drink, your friends, how you spend your time, everything, so that I can be calm, so that I can relax. And tell me when you'll be here.

Your faithful
Samia

★

Sunday, 26 December

I ate in the only restaurant. I asked the man if there were any empty lodgings, even if it were a hole in the ground. He told me the police chief had priority – he wasn't able to bring his family here because he couldn't find anywhere to live. He advised me not to waste my breath: the locals wouldn't take in a bachelor. In the afternoon, the clouds stifled me, so I wandered about aimlessly. I didn't dare take out Samia's letter, which I had been waiting for since I arrived. When I read her delicate handwriting I was ashamed by her lines, and I wept. I resented the colour of the light that infiltrated the empty spaces, I resented the large, closed windows, I resented the men carrying bags of fruit home to their children. The river, like blue copper, drowned me in sorrow. Then I saw the girls of the secondary school in their grey uniforms, and I remembered Samia, and I shivered. It was as though she was looking at me from somewhere I couldn't see: she was far from me, but she was keeping me in view from a hidden place – her face was in the void, watching me and lamenting wherever I went. I nearly threw myself in the river. And I nearly hit the little director when he asked me sharply to pass on to him word for word what was said, and told me I should consider that an order. It was clear to me that he knew exactly what had happened and that he was in secret communication with Abdel-Maqsoud. The office workers cast me mocking looks from behind their files. One of them ordered me a glass of tea. I couldn't fathom the sudden friendliness, and I almost refused it, then at every sip I could feel his gaze: Here I am giving you tea to drink – I'm as good as Abdel-Maqsoud, of course. At the end of the day I asked Uncle Mohamed if he knew of any empty lodgings, but he said it was impossible. Even the shopkeeper, the waiter in the café, shook their heads. They all knew. The men staring at me from the café chairs, the men heading for the station to catch the train too: all of them knew – they had been in on the planning. If I went back to my own city now they would know right away. I told myself I would sleep on the station platform tonight, watching the trains that pass through without stopping. I had a glass of tea, and the talons of small birds tore at my liver. Nightfall would prevent me from returning to the rest-house, and the approaching sunset was like the plague: the houses ejected me into the emptiness that led to the forest of palms.

Youssef

★

'I know full well you've been looking for a lodging-house all day. You thought of going away too. And then in desperation

106

you thought of sleeping on the station platform. But the police would be bound to pick you up. I know you won't find anywhere else – and even if you did, you still wouldn't be able to leave the rest-house. You're here, under my care, and I won't let you want for anything at all. But you have to tell me about everything you do, read me the letters you send to your mother and father... and your friends. If you go to see a film, tell me the story: I haven't been to the cinema for years. And all these books you brought with you – what's in them? Youssef, I've been here for forty years, living in the hope of someone like you coming along – the day you were born I was probably wishing that wish. You and me, from now on: we're one and the same. The whole of the rest-house is at your disposal, even when your official time's over. You'll stay with me. I'm everything to you here. There've been plenty of years when nobody's been in here except the cashier come to give me my monthly salary. Look, I don't even know where the Department office is – but they know where I am.'

★

...I'll tell all and not tell all. Now there's nothing left of me but you. My darling, my letter to you is the only thing I write on the station platform, and who knows, perhaps they'll open it and take it to see what I'm saying to you. My letters to my mother and father and to my friends: I'm expected to read them out loud in exchange for something I can't tell you about, but – it's a force that's certain to bring about my end. Samia, the people here are different, the eyes are different, life is different. I almost cried when I knew at a precise moment that I had not thought about you for an entire day, and your features had faded for me. I'm not lying to you: I'm being completely honest. I'm on the point of running and slapping my own face: my longing for you has brought me to the ground. Even if you sent me your photograph I wouldn't be able to keep it or hang it up anywhere in sight. This thing – if he saw your picture, I'd fear for you: he might track you down, he might go looking for you in our city. He might finish you off like he'll finish me off.

★

'Youssef, give me some money for lunch. Or listen, give me all you've got. What do you need money for? Don't carry anything with you but your pocket money, and you can take that from me every day.'

★

Monday, 17 January
No letters from Samia have reached me for a while. My reply confused her. Now I'm afraid for her. Even if I return to the city, or get a transfer, even if I go back and see the sea every day, will things be as they were between us? Will we run with the same vitality? Laugh? Wonder? Exchange kisses?

★

Wednesday, 19 January
This morning I asked Abdel-Maqsoud for my pocket money, and he took his large wallet out. He said the weather was cold. He said I had screamed twice while I was sleeping, and he had woken me. He was standing a meter away, the blacks of his eyes fixed on me. Outside, the clamor of a train grew louder. He stepped up to me and gripped the back of my neck. His hand was hot, his breath was full of the smell of smoke. I didn't move. I was fettered to the spot by thousands of invisible ties. He put his arm round me and told me he had not stopped dreaming all night of Hosniya, who he had hoped to marry twenty years ago, except that her family had not approved of the match. He said he would not let me go to the office, and drew me back to the room again. The sun

was weak and ineffectual. He was shaking and drooling, unaware of what they would say if I didn't go. He whispered that he would cook pigeon stuffed with green wheat. The clamor of a train grew louder.

★

The director paces back and forth in the room, his hands knotted behind him. He turns in his lower lip, bites it, expels the air hotly from his mouth, and turns to Youssef as if he wants to ask: Is it true, that Mr. Mahrouss said this about him? – as if he doesn't believe it. But he now trusts everything he says: after a few days of Youssef telling Sir every detail, great and small, he shook his hand and confirmed that what he had been telling him was true. How, Youssef did not know – perhaps he had another one of them reporting to him and compared the two accounts. The director spins round suddenly and swears he will have Mr. Mahrouss transferred to the villages on the east bank of the river. Youssef goes out, orders a coffee, pays no heed to their glances. He looks out over the small square through the window next to his desk. How had he dared to report that news to Sir? But it really was what he heard Mr. Mahrouss say: 'Our respected director doesn't satisfy his wife. Have any of you seen her, have you seen the hunger in her eyes?'

★

... so much that – please forgive me – I took the letter to my friend Suad, because she knows about everything between us, but she didn't understand either. She didn't know what to make of it, she said perhaps your sweetheart's in a bind. But what's in your letter is much worse than that. What's happened, my sweet? Is someone threatening you? Have you been kidnapped by gangsters? Has the director done something to harm you? What's happened? Where are our plans for the future? Where are our promises to each other?

★

In the morning he gave him his pocket money, stretched out like a corpse. For four nights he has lain motionless from sunset until Youssef leaves for work, at the end of the night becoming a wild savage, hurting him so much he cries out. Yesterday Youssef almost woke him up, to talk with him, so desperate was his loneliness; he could no longer kill time by reading because Abdel-Maqsoud had piled his books up in the other room – he said they distracted Youssef from him. He stared out of the window, but did not see the men who came to the bridge. Now he is walking along the empty road to the café. The waiter says the town has never seen weather as cold as this. Moments ago he cut across the center of the large square, suddenly sickened, the houses around him silent and sombre – as though the stones had eyes and ears. He was alone through to his marrow, up to the crown of his head. The only footsteps to be heard in the town were his. He ran in the square, and the people peered out from behind the shutters of the windows that gave onto the road. He wanted to scream, to call for anybody – human, djinni, hidden, revealed – to tear him away from these streets, those houses, the café in the midst of emptiness. All that had happened seemed to be happening for the first time. Samia's sad letter was now buried in a drawer in his office. The only thing he feared – who could tell? – was that Abdel-Maqsoud knew everything: some nights ago he asked him assiduously about his relationships with women. Youssef asked himself bitterly why he had troubled to hide the letter from him. If Samia came now. No hopes to build. No soft, whispered conversation to titillate beyond the ears. No kisses. The sea would not enfold their bodies like a tent as they became submerged in it up to their necks. They would not stand in front of furniture shop windows – that corner piece would go well in the living room; Youssef, the sitting room has to be à la mode. It is as though he knows for the first time that he has lost her. Now Samia is a stranger, and his mother too, and his father, and all his distant days in his city washed by the water of the sea. He bites the palm of his hand. He is afraid of seeing Samia suddenly – she will know everything, she will turn and run, and then perhaps he will take her by the hand and lead her to him. It is true, everything is lost.

Youssef stands up. Sharp needles bore into his kidneys. On the corner is a shop selling shaving goods: bottles of scent, razors of all kinds, with red or black handles, behind a dirty glass window. His toes tense inside his shoes, his hands knot together. Abdel-Maqsoud might see it. He will ask him: Why are you carrying it? He learns things quickly – perhaps he is watching him now; perhaps the shop owner knows him. Abdel-Maqsoud will beat him, tear him to pieces, throw him in the canal. No one will know. Uncertainty cuts him in two. The light becomes gloomier, the cold pierces his lungs. A large cloud advances over the houses. He looks up to take in a face of misshapen features and bulging eyes that he might almost have recognized had the wind not swept it quickly away. Suddenly, the shop owner comes out and says, staring up at the sky: 'Rain never falls here.'

Translated from the Arabic by R. Neil Hewison

LIVERPOOL JOHN MOORES UNIVERSITY
LEARNING SERVICES

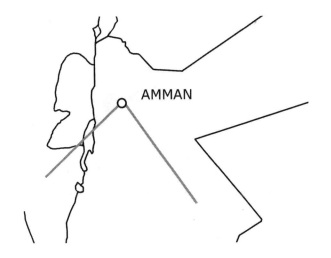
AMMAN

Amman's Birds Sweep Low

ELIAS FARKOUH

1. The Beginning

In the early evening, Amman's sunset horizon is an astonishing, bleeding cloud. A small cluster of mountains blazes as if – seen from a distance – they were a gem just plucked from the dirt. They are silent and distant, but visible whichever way you look.

The first man said, 'Let's go.'

The woman asked, 'Where?'

Their friend who owned the car (whose only previous contact with his passengers was cultural soirées) suggested, 'Let's raid the other side of town. I'll introduce you to it.'

So they shot off.

Amman's streets, crowded with flesh and faces, were as congested as a winding passageway after the Ramadan *iftar*. Lights from the sidewalk and closed shops flashed over the transient chunk of metal. The glare of a second awakening lent its colour to the city, which was emerging from its daily sauna. They were in the fracas, sliding in their vehicle through a forest of mobile metal, and shot away.

There were five of them. The car's owner turned to his right, where Nisreen sat. Addressing everyone, he declared, 'It's an invasion, my dears.'

The woman retorted, 'And you're our commander?'

She laughed, and her laughter sounded stingingly bitter, despite her hoarseness or because of it.

He replied, 'The bourgeoisie lead, and everyone else follows, Nisreen. That's history.'

She parried, as if brushing aside an expert lie, 'That may hold true for a commander, since a commander is someone who has shed his social class.'

'How about me?'

From the back seat, Ibrahim observed, 'You're the car owner. Show us the other side's wonders.'

They left behind them the 3rd Circle and began to enter West Amman's outskirts. The streets were wide and allowed the car to speed up. The vehicle's phosphorescent speedometer crept to eighty and then a hundred. The night air licked their faces, and a childish delight overwhelmed them. So they surrendered to the silence and to the intoxication of the forthcoming exploration.

2. Identities and Characteristics

They advanced into the night. In the heart of the new Amman, their searching eyes peered at the sights, both the illuminated ones and those gone dark. Once they left the area of Amman they knew, a profound stillness took hold of them.

'Even their air is purer and cleaner!' Titi said with astonishment as a strand of her hair flapped like a flag.

(Her name, Nefertiti, became Titi, which is shorter and cuter. Her facial features suggested a mix of Circassian blood (from her mother) and Arab (from her late father). She was in community college and loved her fiancé Khalaf, who had drilled her in political theory till she adopted his ideology. She was thin, perhaps because she couldn't get enough to eat. Her mother's dinars scarcely met her needs and those of her three brothers. Her jeans, however, were tight and suited her perfectly.)

They went slowly down a dark side street, where the only light came from the car's headlights, which penetrated the gloom with two streams of light. The crunch of gravel from the road, which was not paved, broke the silence. The driver slowed down, and the car slithered between the elegant, darkened houses. Looking around, they were dazzled. They had never seen such beautiful architecture before.

Stopping before a house bathed in light, the car's owner whispered, 'What great engineering and design!'

Nisreen, as if pouncing on his words to toss them back at him, commented, 'Engineering, like science, is value-neutral until it serves someone.'

(In her forties, she was a widow who had learned from her husband only procreation and how to drop a rung or two on the social ladder. What she had retained – reading, debating, a taste for the music of Beethoven, Bach, and Chopin – could be traced back to her early years. Her face still revealed some remnants of her former beauty. Her slender fingers' tremor did not prevent her from writing feminist essays, which helped to support her.)

'That's enough commentary, woman. Beauty can't endure your analysis,' the car's owner protested. Pointing into the semi-darkness, he added, 'See how the wall's masonry matches the wide balcony.'

Khalaf laughed and – with a wink toward the car's owner – commented, 'He's interested in walls and how they harmonize with balconies – amazing! How did you detect that, even though we can't see a thing in this darkness?'

Riled, he responded, 'I've seen it by daylight.'

From the back seat Ibrahim guffawed crazily and said sarcastically, 'Ha, ha; are you following your dream, my dear? You'll never achieve it. They won't let you rise.'

'I'll achieve it in spite of them. You'll see,' the car owner replied tersely to their mocking remarks.

Suddenly Ibrahim exclaimed, 'Keep it down! I see

people.'

They noticed more than one head through the wide window, several of them. The figures seemed to be studying the automobile and its occupants, who squirmed in its seats and then huddled together, their mouths opening and closing soundlessly. Some invisible force stretched between the two clusters of heads, inside the house and out, creating a hideous link with an intense electric jolt.

A suspenseful calm gripped the car's occupants while they watched the heads in the window. The car's interior was still. Night and silence circled the vehicle, visited the street, the wall, the illuminated garden, and even surrounded the heads. The sights came into focus.

The chamber glowed white, and a stupendous, dazzling, branched chandelier hung over the small heads that moved mutely. Ibrahim muttered almost ecstatically, 'My God! Only mosques have chandeliers like that!'

(He was a low-ranking clerk in a bank. They used to tell him, 'You'll never get a promotion, Ibrahim. Your sarcastic presence provokes them; all they want is obedience.' He was one of many displaced by the 1967 war. He and his mother fled from Jericho and saw death first hand in al-Khan al-Ahmar.[1] He had a complex, which he never tired of exaggerating when he discussed the war: 'The war! Which war? We'll never fight a war. That's what Bourguiba said when he saw the stately homes on the West Bank. We assailed him, calling him a traitor, but when the war came we fled. We were no better than he was.')

Inside the garden a dog barked a number of times. Then it placed its front paws on the low gate. Ibrahim responded by poking his head out the window and barking like a dog, 'Wow, wow, woowoowow, son of a bitch!'

1. Al-Khan al-Ahmar - battlefield during the June War of 1967, in the western part of the Jordan valley.

Then he released a loud and lengthy peal of laughter. Khalaf, who recognized its abnormal character, told him, 'Stop. That isn't laughter; it's a wail.'

He saw that Ibrahim's eyes were filling with tears. Two streams flowed down his face before uniting. Part of Khalaf's mouth quivered, and his fingers pressed Titi's shoulder.

(A tawny Bedouin from al-Mafraq, he was characterized by an innate poise and wariness, which made him seem older than he was. His face suggested the desert's harsh aridity and contrasted with his fiancée, whose urbanity suggested succulence, as did the smooth features of her face. He was posted to a forgotten spot, which was desiccated by the southern sun. His desk was in a tin hut with a placard on its door that read: 'Customs Authority.')

Ibrahim asked him once with deliberate sarcasm, 'What do you customize?'

Trying to jettison his typical caution, Khalaf replied, 'The wind, dirt, and smuggled cigarettes.'

'Then you all have your work cut out for you; God bless you. But how about banned books?'

'I read them.'

'Take care, friend. They'll accuse you of encouraging the smugglers.'

The car's engine roared into action after the dog went crazy and almost broke its chain. They had just left behind the lighted house when the car's wheels hit a solid obstruction and vibrated.

'What's that?' the fiancée shouted.

The car's owner said confidently, as though he really knew, 'Potholes belonging to the people who own houses in this neighbourhood.'

'Private potholes in a public street!' the clerk exclaimed as his eyes stole a parting glance at the clear, white illumination, which was fading into the distance, sinking into a gloom as quiet as a cemetery.

3. On the Mandalun Heights

They were diving into the city's night while Amman, with steel talons, etched its new landmarks on their souls. There were so many private potholes that the car's owner worried about their effect on his vehicle. Even so he said, 'In a minute you'll see something spectacular.'

The woman objected, 'We've seen enough. We're not masochists. And you – I wonder if you're a sadist?'

He ignored her remark and decided to go all out. 'It's a boil this night must lance,' he murmured without anyone hearing him.

The area spread before them in all its naked darkness, except for a well of light here and there. To the left, in the distant gloom, a minaret rose, bathed in green light. Several hundred meters below them a red word in Latin letters shone in the dark sky: 'Mandalun.'

'What's this Mandalun?' the clerk asked without his usual sarcasm.

'A public venue. A restaurant or club.'

'Public! I've never heard of it before. My friend, it looks private. Have you been inside?'

The vehicle's owner replied, 'Not yet. I'll do that some day.' Then he stopped the car.

Everyone stared at the strange building, which was situated between piles of rock and huge steel shipping containers. When the driver opened his door, a shadow fell on their faces, increasing the strangeness. He turned on the headlights, which were aimed at the structure, and then got out, heading toward it. The others piled out and caught up with him. He stopped, and they did too, looking around anxiously. The building loomed before them. It rose, climbing high, in the darkness. A wall ran to the right till it reached the entry façade. There, at its base, successive sets of steps disappeared into the interior gloom.

The fiancée demanded, 'What's this?'

The Bedouin replied, 'A monument.'

'No,' objected the woman. 'A mansion.'

Then the clerk pronounced his verdict, 'It's a fortress. Don't you see the small slits at the top? A huge building like this has got to be a fort.'

The shadows they cast on this building's giant façade lengthened in a peculiar way. The car's owner moved, saying, 'Follow me; you'll see.'

They had only taken a few steps when a man with a torch appeared – the night watchman. The car's owner took him aside and then gestured for them to enter. So they did.

High, concrete stairways led to an upper floor with sharp angles and narrow corners. More than one interior balcony overlooked what lay beneath. There was a cistern below, with marble bands, but dirt and cement were piled in it. From there, a narrow corridor led to the building's lowest level. Light bulbs, dangling at intervals, lent the place a special kind of terror.

'What is this? A house or something else?'

One of them said, 'It's a strange house, but why is it so huge?'

'It's not merely huge; look at the security systems on the inside walls. This house is like a fortress.'

Through a narrow slit, the clerk looked out at the expansive view and shouted, 'Come. From here a person can see even a mouse moving among the rocks.'

They all gathered around an opening. Quivering with lights that danced in the middle of the pitch blackness, Amman revealed one of its aspects. The clerk performed a countdown at the aperture, extending first his left arm and then the right. He yelled, 'Bang, bang, boom, buzz... watch for incoming shells. Rush to the other slits. It's an attack. They're attacking our house itself!'

They exploded with raucous laughter, which ricocheted through the empty house. Then they calmed down a little, as if the game had caught their fancy. They split into two teams and spread out in the shadows, down the stairways and in the corners. The Bedouin screamed, 'Attaaaaack!'

Other voices followed, 'Bang, buzz, boom. Roarrrr! Fire the mortar. Let's go, brother. I've been hit by shrapnel. Take cover, Ibrahim. Nisreen here is aiming her rifle at you. Titi, you traitor; I've found you. You're on the other side! It's easy to bribe vacillators. No, a Bedouin is never duplicitous. A Bedouin is true to his word. Ibrahim, watch out! They're closing in on you from both sides of the river. Withdraw to the desert; it will shelter you. Never mind; your position in the muddy alleys is secure now. Aye, you've been stabbed, Nisreen. No, it's Titi. Help Ibrahim, Titi. And you, Nisreen. Hurry to the second line of defence. Bang! Time to advance. Advance! Buzz, boom.'

Roles became confused and the teams' players merged, defending but then attacking; friends and then enemies. A red flag in a corner and a black banner in an alcove. Kharijis versus Umayyads. Carmatians versus Abbasids. Colonizers versus the colonized. Oppressors and the oppressed. Rich and poor. Zionists and Arabs; Arabs and Arabs.

They pursued each other to the ground floor, where the Bedouin stumbled on a doorstep, swayed, and fell on the entry stairs.

His fiancée rushed to him, yelling, 'I'm not a traitor or a vacillator.'

The woman disappeared behind the concrete basin and began firing on the clerk, who was hiding in the shadow of one of the huge steel containers.

Suddenly the fiancée screamed, 'That's enough. Khalaf's hurt.'

Her tone was grave this time. The clerk and the woman stopped and hurried over to the Bedouin's body, which lay in a heap on the steps. His hands cradled his wounded knee, and his trousers were torn. He laughed nervously to hide his pain and said, 'It's nothing, just a flesh wound. Is the battle over?'

The woman smiled and said as she leaned over his knee, 'It's over, even before it began. We're all fine. We're all on the same side.'

After one of the scouts flushed him out, the car's owner appeared suddenly and shouted, 'What about me? Whose side am I on? Winners' or losers'?'

The clerk rose. A faint rustling in the sky had attracted his attention. He looked up and spotted with difficulty a flock of delicate wings sweeping low toward Amman, which quivered in the night.

The car's owner drew closer to the steps, repeating his question, pretending to bellow, 'What about me?'

Some distance away, the clerk, who was still watching the wings fly past, replied, 'Didn't I tell you? You're the car owner.'

Translated by William Maynard Hutchins

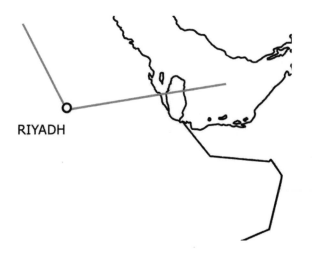

RIYADH

There's No Room for a Lover in this City

YOUSEF AL-MOHAIMEED

I know very well that the postal services in my city are a bit like my grandfather's dilapidated mud wall but I never expected them to be so tardy that a letter would arrive one year and four months after it was posted. My God! Which drawer had it been stuck in all that time? Whose fiendish fingers strangled this love and passion for so long? Who concealed my letter for such an age?

I spotted them in their GMC combing Laila Al-Akhyaliya Street. They'd just turned off Arouba Road and were suspiciously scanning the interior of The Blue Diamond video store in case a recalcitrant woman had transgressed and snuck into a shop that sold films. They stopped their car with the emblem of the commission that struck terror and apprehension into peoples' hearts emblazoned upon its door. Two men with small pot bellies alighted, cleaning their teeth with toothpicks in slow robotic motions. They wore short thobes[1] and shabby black shoes, and the shmagh[2] of one had slid back across the top of his head. Grim faced, they entered a shop which sold flowers and wedding paraphernalia and proceeded to search the cold

---

1. Thobe - ankle-length robe with long sleeves worn by some Arab men.
2. Shmagh - a man's headcloth, of thicker material than the ghutra, and most commonly with a red chequered pattern.

cabinet that was full of roses of assorted colours. One of them
ordered the Syrian sales assistant to put all the red ones in a
box, which the other one then put into the back of the car.

And on they moved, one following the other, entering
each shop and leaving it, like a needle and thread profaning
cloth. How mixed up this crazy city is: one minute panting
after love, only to hunt it down the next, banning red roses on
the feast of lovers, cursing Mr. Valentine from the pulpit on
Fridays and warning of wantonness and debauchery.

I could feel their madness and indignation as they set
upon the Bangladeshi workers in the satellite shops, rummaging
through drawers for cards for porn channels and confiscating
receivers. Their sinister car made a turn at the traffic lights at
Al-Jazeera Supermarket, before pulling up in 'Lucifer Street'
– their name for it, alluding to its sin and godlessness. As they
approached, one of the Bangladeshi shopkeepers gave a signal
and immediately all the Indian, Bengali and Pakistani salesmen
concealed their secret wares.

That's how they operate; snatching red roses, and satellite
transmission equipment; taking mobile phones off suspicious
looking passers-by so they can check them out for signs of
some mischief or other. But letters? Would they really go so
far as to snoop on ordinary letters in the mail? Had her letter
been with them all that time? I didn't think so. If it had it
would never have arrived at all. Or at least I would have
noticed something to suggest that it had been opened, and if
they had done that they could just as easily have delivered it
directly to my mail box, and then set a cunning ambush for
me in the souq so they could arrest me and flog me in their
headquarters, or publicly in the souq.

I opened the little pink envelope for the twentieth time
and contemplated the handwriting. It resembled silver
necklaces, small and decorative, a little shaky. I read the last
sentence: 'Please don't forget darling, I beg you.' Forget what?
I said to myself. Shit! Do I go and meet you now, after all this
time has passed? Surely you're not still going there every week
waiting for me to turn up, unless you're completely bonkers!

I sat at my table, which was pushed against the wall, and looked up at all the bits of paper and their words of love. In the first letter she had written: 'To the man with the three apples, I love you. That's it!' At the time I had been coming back to my humble room from my weekly shop, carrying a plastic bag with three green apples in it. She spotted me from the window of the house opposite. All I saw was a dark shadow against the frosted glass with a yellow lamp behind it. Then I found the piece of paper. How wonderful it was for a village lad like me who had come to this huge crazy shameless city, to see the silhouette of a woman dancing with the dim light of the pale yellow lamp behind her.

From the moment I set foot in this city to pursue my studies I never seemed to have a permanent address. I'd rent a room for a month or two but it was very rare that the delightful ring of a telephone would break its deadly silence. And if ever I was lucky enough to find somewhere with a line to link me with the outside world and the sweet breathing and poignant pauses of a woman's conversation, the landlord would soon kick me out for one reason or another; the most serious being my lateness with the monthly rent, the most trivial the claims of a rustic neighbour that I was a single man of dubious character who didn't pray with the congregation in the mosque. In fact I was the first to set foot in the mosque and mine the last tongue to cease uttering supplication and requests for divine forgiveness, but the neighbour had it in for me because he came home one day bringing his three daughters back from school and found me standing in the street. He didn't stop at his own door but continued driving up and down the alley until I went inside, just so I wouldn't see his daughters who were completely covered up by their abbayas[3] anyway.

When I finally managed to obtain my own post office box, having paid the three hundred riyal fee, I was so delighted

3. Abbaya - a long black garment worn by women over their clothes covering from neck to toe.

that I nearly crashed into a huge lorry. My old Corolla 88 almost ended up under the wheels of the speeding juggernaut with me splayed stupidly across the radiator like a fragile insect.

Once, when my friends at the university were trying to contact me, one of them asked where I was living, and how they could visit. 'He's a man of no fixed abode,' another quipped sarcastically. The morning I took possession of my own post box, I met the three of them by the fountain in front of the arts faculty. 'Now, you bastards,' I announced in a loud vindictive voice, 'I've got a permanent address in this crazy God-forsaken city of yours.' Students passing by turned to look in silent disapproval at my unruly behaviour on the solemn university campus.

Yes, now I can keep in touch with the world thanks to that magic mail box, and no one in the world can take it away from me. True, letters can go astray, or lie unnoticed for several months. They may get opened sometimes and then resealed shoddily, but in the end they arrive, limp, dizzy and defaced. I opened the old letter again and contemplated the three lines, and the signature and the broken hearts in the corners of the page and the hijra[4] date and the day.

I quickly read the lines: 'I'll wait for you next Friday, six in the evening, Andalus shopping centre. Do you know it? On the stone bench in front of Arabian Perfumes. If you can't make it, or you don't get this letter in time, make it the Friday after next. Agreed? I have to see you. My fate hangs in the balance!'

Good grief! How many Fridays have passed since then? I tried to count them but stopped: were Fridays like the flocks of pigeons that passed above my head, flock by flock just before the sun awakes when all I can hear is the intermittent flapping of their wings, then they're gone, leaving no trace. It

4. Hijra - the Islamic calendar.

was a Wednesday. I gazed at the wall of my small room in Hayy Al-Maseef. The calendar looked back at me mockingly as if to say: 'Call yourself a lover. Look how many Fridays you've wasted!'

In my humble lodging I did not possess a telephone to link me up with any voice to put the night to flight and chase away the cockroaches that shared the room with me and were forever landing upside down inside my shoe. I had tried to call her from the phone boxes on Aleesha Street and Al-Fakhiriya Street. For days there had been no answer, then the recorded message: 'The number you have dialed is incorrect, please make sure you have the correct number.' I had been desperately sad and afraid when we lost touch completely.

I decided to visit Andalus Shopping Centre and check it out before the following Friday came. After visiting a friend in Hayy Al-Maseef I drove south down Olaya Street and crossed the junction at King Abdullah Road. The Sheraton Hotel on the corner slumbered nervously behind concrete security barriers. As I waited at the lights just before the shopping centre I could see Kingdom Tower, a sixty floor monstrosity standing ugly and imposing as it looked down on insignificant me with the haughtiness of the mighty. I pulled up in front of Andalus, got out of the car and took a cautious walk around. I scoured the place from every angle before sitting down on the blackened stone bench. Then I got back in the car and did a U-turn at the intersection with Arouba Street where I got caught up among the shoppers coming out of Smaa discount store with their cheap purchases.

Friday evening, a full hour before six, I put on my thobe and shmagh, and a splash of cheap perfume which made me cough all the way to the rendezvous. I knew that more than sixteen months had passed, more than sixty weeks and Fridays, four hundred and twenty days. What madness! Do you think she's been waiting for you, Mr. Don Juan, every Friday for all that time, I whispered to myself. Am I really crazy? I touched the spot on the back of my neck where it had been burned with an iron rod a long time ago, when I was a child about seven years old. I recalled how I used to collect stones at that time. I had started to hide them in the cupboard under the stairs without anyone realizing what I was up to. After a year I had amassed a collection of many different kinds of stones. I spent some wonderful nights with them. I loved them, was in raptures over them. I talked to them. I swear I could hear their soft voices whispering. I kissed them and fell out with them. I would set them out in neat little rows and arrange a place for each one to rest. I interacted with the stones remarkably well and was delighted with their colours, shapes and spirits. I even gave them names and ages and characteristics. My stones belonged to tribes and families. I don't know, but perhaps tribes and families are merely stones. My stones, however, had souls and breathed. They also made hidden noises that only I could hear. I wasn't crazy. It was just that I was like a wild animal, smelling and hearing what others cannot smell and hear.

There was one particular little stone which I called Dimwit. He was black and had a huge head and small body. Every time I put him somewhere, the next night I'd find he'd moved somewhere else or retreated to some distant crack under the stairs where my hand couldn't reach him. I would have to lay flat on my young belly and crawl like a mischievous viper so that I could pull him out and give him a good telling off: 'Why are you playing the fool, running away from me? You're setting a bad example and encouraging the others to escape.'

One day, while she was cleaning the house, my mother discovered the hiding place under the stairs. She didn't say a word, didn't tell me off or shout at me. In fact I didn't know she'd come across my beloved world of stones until I came home from school in the afternoon. I jumped out of my thobe and retreated to my lost world under the stairs. It was empty. My father had removed the stones and thrown them away. I screamed hysterically and hit the walls wildly. 'Why,

Dimwit? Why did you run away with them? Why did you do it, Dimwit? You traitor!' I thought that it was the stone, Dimwit, who had led the escape back into the desert. My mother rushed over, saying bismillah[5] over and over again, and took me in her arms. My father was alarmed when he heard me screaming. As soon as he heard the reason for my ranting he thought I was calling him a dimwit and a traitor. He didn't know I was screaming at my beautiful black stone and he set about me, punching and kicking me. My mother had quite some difficulty in releasing me from his grip and she ran with me up to the roof. I was ill for days afterwards and gradually began to loose my sight until I could no longer see properly. I would lean against the wall and feel my way for the drawer or the door. All I could make out were foggy images of the things around me. I stopped going to school.

Then one miserable evening my eldest uncle visited us. He convinced my father: 'The lad's possessed.' What I needed were some sessions of Quran reading with the imam of the local mosque. After the imam had heard my story he confirmed to my father that a heathen idol-worshipping genie had possessed me and made me fall in love with stones to the extent that I was obsessed. The imam began to visit us at home. He would grab hold of me and bring his face right up to mine as he muttered verses from the Quran and blow his foul breath, accompanied by a drizzle of saliva, in my face. I would turn away to avoid the disgusting smell but he would force my head back towards him as he informed my father that it was the genie inside me that was twisting my neck because it was terrified of Allah's verses. After a number of visits reciting and blowing on my face and chest hadn't worked the imam advised that I should be shown to a traditional healer in Manfouha who treated patients by burning with hot iron.

---

5. Bismillah - in the name of Allah.

On the way there I sat between my father, who was driving his small truck, and my uncle who was in the passenger seat. My hands were ice cold like a corpse's. I could hear them talking but didn't understand a thing they were saying. All I can remember was the main street in Manfouha, the shops and hawkers, the Indians and old women selling spices on the pavement, and the local buses parked in a small square near the old Al-Asha well. We entered a dark narrow alley in the heart of Manfouha where small half naked children were playing football. My father pulled up and my uncle took me by my icy hands and lifted me out of the car. They led me into the dark corridor of a traditional old house. The door was green iron and the steps blackened by passing feet and the backsides of women sitting while they waited for their turn with the sheikh. The men's room was small and packed with patients. When we entered the sheikh was sitting cross legged on the floor next to a burning brazier and a pot of Arab coffee. A lad walked among the customers with tiny patterned china cups, which he pulled from a bowl of water that had gone green from the dregs of coffee. As he poured he lifted the pot into the air before offering the cup to the person accompanying the patient. The sheikh asked my uncle how he was while he heated up an iron rod on the fire. Then he sat me down next to him and repeated: 'Mashaa'allah[6], mashaa'allah, young man!' He felt the back of my little neck, his thumb and index finger squeezing the skin so hard that I winced with the pain: 'Ouch!' When he pulled my hair I tried to run away and cried but my father gripped my waist between his two strong legs and my uncle held my head in front of the sheikh. The sheikh placed the white hot iron lightly on the back of my neck and the room shuddered at the short shriek accompanied by the smell of burning flesh and wisps of white smoke. Then he did

---

6. Mashaa'allah - what Allah wills, an utterance of approval, or to counter against envy.

the same thing again, just under my left ear.

I felt the back of my neck and under my ear as I parked my little car on Olaya Street, in front of the ATM machine to be precise, opposite the Andalus. The clock said ten minutes to six. There weren't too many people in the centre; some women carrying bags of shopping, dragging their kids behind them. Other kids were holding on to their mothers' abbayas and crying. A few Bangladeshis moved among the shoppers distributing leaflets. Young men collecting donations, light hair on their chins like drought stricken grass, were shouting: 'Give generously to your brothers in Chechnya. Charity doesn't diminish your money but only makes it grow.' Smartly dressed Syrian and Lebanese shop assistants stood at the doors of their stores waiting for customers. Some of them slunk back inside nervously when they spotted the Commission man with his dark woolen cloak and thick beard. He was followed like a shadow by two policemen and was repeating his mantra: 'Cover yourself up woman, cover yourself up sister, veil your eyes, girl!' I got in a muddle myself when I saw him, and decided to seek shelter, like a mouse, in a men's clothes shop. I emerged with a plastic bag hoping it would contribute to my credibility as I wandered around the mall. I had felt obliged to buy a skull cap and two pairs of socks I didn't need just so I could carry a bag and give the impression I was a genuine shopper and not just someone who had wandered in off the street. Out of the corner of my eye I noticed the stone benches. A woman was sitting on one of them with a tiny baby in her arms. I looked at the time. It was exactly six o'clock. I became confused and my heart beat so fast it almost jumped through my ribcage and landed on the tiled floor. I approached her and walked slowly by the side of the bench. I could see her eyes lined with black kohl peering from behind her niqab[7]. I passed her and then turned to look back. Her eyes were watching me. Good God, is it really her? It can't be! After sixty Fridays spent waiting devotedly every six o'clock? I decided to go back again, but should I pass next to her, or should I be brave, impudent even, and sit down next to her? Wasn't the stone seat wide enough for three people? There was no one else there and she was sitting on the end of the seat. That's true, I said to myself, but here's no room for a lover in this city!

As I approached her I suddenly remembered her little pink envelope. I'll get it out and hold it in my left hand, which will be directly in front of her. Perhaps she would remember the envelope. Sixty Fridays is not long enough to forget such a letter, not if it was going to decide her fate, as she claimed. But who was that baby in her arms? Had she gotten married and given birth in a year and four months? Perhaps our appointment really had been a matter of destiny for her? As I walked past with my pink letter in the hand nearest to her I realized that her eyes were brimming with consternation. She shifted suddenly as if she were about to get up and follow me. Was it really the woman I was in love with? Or had she simply been perturbed by the envelope because she thought I was a young man on the make who wanted to hand her his phone number before disappearing to wait by the telephone for days. I hurried on. I could feel her footsteps behind me. I turned round suddenly. She was following me. I set off across the car park towards my car on Olaya Street. She turned after me but then she stopped. I looked round to find her getting into a fancy new car. I stood by my car motionless. As her car passed I saw her eyes looking towards me. She even turned her head to look back as the car pulled away. I raised my hand and waved. Then suddenly I spotted the Commission man and the two policemen leaving the centre in their GMC with the emblem of the Commission for the Promulgation of Virtue and the Prevention of Vice inscribed on the vehicle's door.

I went back to the stone bench in case she'd left

7. Niqab - a full veil covering the entire face, with a slit for the eyes.

something there for me. I sat in exactly the same place she had been sitting in. I inspected the seat and bent my neck to explore the tiles underneath it. I spotted a hair band that was also pink. I picked it up and smelled it. I looked to my right at the trunk of a large poinciana tree that was just next to the bench. I remembered a strange story my grandmother used to tell me before I went to sleep, about a man traveling through the desert. He heard a soft sad moaning sound. After searching a while for the source of the sound he realized it was coming from a large awsaj[8] tree. He walked up to it and heard it say: 'Release me, release me!' 'How?' he asked, but the tree just repeated the same words: 'Release me, release me!' He pulled out his knife and made a mark on the trunk of the tree. All of a sudden it turned into a woman of astounding beauty. 'I belong to you now,' she said to him, and added, 'An envious and spiteful genie turned me into a tree and told me: 'Only an artist or a poet shall release you.''

I took my keys out of my pocket and carved a heart and two eyes. No sooner had I stood up than I heard a rustling sound behind me as a woman of astounding beauty came up to me and whispered in my ear: 'I will live with you, even in the cupboard under the stairs.' I swear I could hear her and I spoke to her, although many of those around me couldn't see her with me. Like roots and branches her delicate slender fingers entwined with my trembling fingers and off we walked together.

I spent the following days cruising the streets of Riyadh in amazement. There weren't many people out and about and as I looked through the car window at the few trees by the side of the road, I smiled to myself because I alone know how

8. Awsaj - a tree with large thorns and small red berries which can reach three metres in height. Pigeons and other birds take refuge in it from hawks and falcons. The Bedouin, who call its berries 'wolves' blood', believe it is inhabited by jinn, or genies, and do not chop its wood for fuel. They throw stones at it when they pass and say 'Bismillah'.

to make them follow me wherever I go. When we are alone I hug and embrace them and we sleep together and enjoy exquisite pleasure and unbridled passion.

Translated from the Arabic by Anthony Calderbank

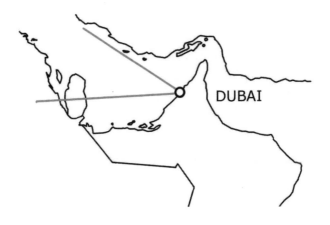

DUBAI

The Week Before the Wife Arrived

FADWA AL-QASEM

Friday 14th September

Task until next summer: painstakingly rebuild enough inner peace to maintain at least borderline quality of life.

By Thursday night he had succumbed to the feeling of defeat. Now he knew for certain that his life would completely collapse. He knew he was doomed as soon as he saw her at the arrivals hall at the Dubai International Airport. The way she had pinched her nose and sniffed; he knew that the stench of honeyed tobacco had powerfully invaded her nostrils. What he thought was a tightly knit fabric of cover-ups had already started to unravel as a tiny thread got caught on the baggage trolley they abandoned haphazardly outside the airport.

He watched himself open the door for her and the kids. He watched himself get into the car and sit behind the wheel. Spanish classical flamenco music floated around in his head. Long fingers softly, slowly, quietly strumming the guitar strings. The melody swept through his soul, leaving a deafening silence to invade his thoughts, warning him of the crescendo to come. The same tune repeated itself again and again, but was getting faster, louder, faster, louder...

She looked for a long time at both his hands on the

steering wheel. One was obviously much darker than the other. His palms were hot and clammy. His contribution to the conversation was just as clammy. When she reached for his mobile to call a friend, he nearly snatched it from her hand. He tried very hard to remember if he had deleted Titiana's name and the messages she had sent him in his wife's absence, and whether or not he had in fact thrown out the condoms.

He knew she was already recording his every move in that little book with endless pages residing inside her head. Many years ago her attention to detail was one of the characteristics that drew him to her. He had been greatly, but secretly, flattered by the way she was attentive to everything he said and everything he left unsaid. She would remember things he had long taken for granted; the dimples on his cheeks when he smiled; the green flickers of colour in his eyes when the sun shone on his face. Things like how he preferred his tea light with one and a half teaspoons of sugar, while he drank his coffee well boiled and bitter; that he liked his water very cold; and the fact that she had always remembered to bring him some chocolate to eat before smoking shisha.

As they drove into the car park of their apartment building, he noticed with much relief, and much greater guilt, that there was a new watchman crouching on his haunches smoking a cigarette. But he knew that this, too, would not go unnoticed.

Thursday 13th September

Change wife's name back from Nabil in mobile contacts list.
Delete Titiana's name and messages.

He kept putting off removing her name and number, although he had already deleted all her inspiring, regenerating messages. Just having her name amongst his list of contacts was enough to keep alight the embers of his belief in himself as a man. It was like a tiny crack in the huge wall he stared at each day that reminded him again and again of his disappointments. A tiny crack in that obstinate wall, letting in enough sunshine to briefly warm his heart.

Wednesday 12th September

Delete recent items on desktop, internet cache and internet browsing history.

Everything everywhere reeked of tobacco; it was getting to him. He felt it making him delirious. He looked around the building for the watchman, but he saw only Khan's things; his frayed and faded laundry hanging on a plastic coated wire knotted on two rusty nails, his tool kit, his bicycle, his eyes.

The streets were lined with cars. The car parks were full. The parking meters on the pavements were shimmering orange in the sun. He parked on the sand on a plot of land which will probably be turned into yet another 'tallest building'. He parked unconcerned as to whether he would be trapped by other cars. He'll deal with that when it occurs. He called in sick. He took his laptop and walked to The French Connection. One café latte and he sat there for hours, hooked up to the net, surfing, looking for nothing.

Tuesday 11th September

Bring someone to clean-up the house.

The tobacco odour was fast spreading throughout the city. As he drove to his office this morning it appeared to be forming a thick, heavy fog hiding the tips of unfinished sky scrapers lining Sheikh Zayed Road. The winds carried soft golden sands into every crevice possible, reminding him once more that this city resides in a vast open desert hidden behind rows of tall mirrored towers planted along the road. Like him, these buildings succeeded in superficially blending in – perhaps temporarily, perhaps permanently. Time will be the final judge. For now, they are all here, he thought, their roots extending upwards to the frivolous fog.

He felt no strong attachment to any country, and this one was no exception. The image of rooting to nothing but the sky pleased him. It made him feel like the free-spirited persona he projected himself as in front of others; although his wife, of course, never glimpsed this version of him.

Since he got married, some ten years ago, he had avoided doing any housework whatsoever. Within weeks he had established the ground rules – and she had accepted them all, for it was he who had saved her from the life sentence of spinsterhood one month before she entered her 34th year. She was pretty and intelligent, but her arrogance had slowly twisted into an abhorrent conceit, a haughtiness which kept even female friendships at bay. Over the years insistent clicking of tongues had broken her spirit, turning her into a contortionist whose only aim was to please everyone. A silent, desperate creature learning to accept a life thinly tied to the fragile hope of potential suitors who would come from far away lands, because this city of dreams had not yielded the desired one.

It truly must have been one weak moment when he eventually gave in to his mother's constant nagging. His mind must have been very foggy when he decided to actually get married, although, like the majority of his male peers, he thought himself a good catch. He was 38, his life was as uncomplicated as his bachelor's apartment was cluttered. If there was something wrong in his life, he would have never guessed it.

When he arrived at his apartment building, he headed straight for the management office and ranted and raged about Khan's peeping as if it had happened just yesterday and not two years ago. Management was unaware of his wife's traveling, and he knew with a pang of guilt, that Khan did not stand a chance.

Monday 10th September

Wean off single friends.

The bucket of water he threw down the drain yesterday had apparently seeped out some corroded pipes. The odour of the tobacco was now all over the small building in which he lived. He was lost as to what he could do about it. But Khan's increasingly threatening stares he *would* do something about. The last thing he needed was this guy telling his wife that he had seen him with another woman. The hell he would go through to convince her that nothing had happened was not worth it precisely because nothing had happened!

The first summer his wife went to Amman, they had kissed each other goodbye. They had at least cared for one another. Despite the circumstances of their marriage, he counted the days till her return – though never openly in front of his friends. It was the manly thing to rejoice at the prospect of returned bachelorhood. Suddenly his friends would regain their courage and bombard him almost daily with pleas to go somewhere. It was an annual ritual they all seemed to look forward to, one from which no one appeared able to escape once entangled in the nets of the Arabian Gulf. It never mattered where they went – popular and simple shisha cafes, dodgy night clubs and bars – it was the act of defiance and the exhilaration that came with it that mattered.

Yet another message from Titiana; the vibration announcing the message's arrival sent shivers down his spine. How is it that we take stock of everything in our lives but not our lives? He tried hard to remember the feeling he used to have when it was his wife he thought of whenever he felt an emotional intensity as they watched a movie together or listened to a moving piece of music. Violin music in particular always stirred his passion; the soulfulness, the tenderness, the smoothness. It would make him feel vibrant, alive, desirable.

145

He would take her hand, his senses heightened, and lead her to bed. He would be on fire, yearning for the pleasures of sex. It was only years later that he discovered the reason he was never quite fulfilled was that he had always been the only one hearing the violins.

He forgot now how often they had sat there staring at the TV wearing intimate clothing but no longer sharing any intimate moments; she no longer felt or smelt the same. Stealthily did that moment arrive, he cannot pinpoint it now, when the relief he felt was stronger than the pain of loss, when his carelessness overwhelmed his emotional need for her. As long as life was somehow running its course, it was easier to just let it keep on running. The memory of how things were before was simply becoming too heavy a burden to continue shouldering, it was easier to put down the load, as each summer they bid each other goodbye with one less kiss.

These days what he truly cherished was his time alone in his car; sometimes he could even have complete thoughts and develop his own philosophies. Sometimes he would park his car somewhere, turn the music on so loud it would exorcise everything else from his system, then he would just sit there watching people rushing around. He would study their facial expressions, the way they swung their arms, the colour of their socks. He never tried to picture their lives, he just tried to imagine what they might be thinking at that precise moment when he became aware of their existence. There's an intoxicating feeling of power watching others while you yourself remain motionless, serene, detached, free of the burden of compassion. He made up his mind – Khan must go.

Sunday 9th September

Continue tanning left hand with wedding ring on.
Increase efforts to get rid of honeyed tobacco smell.

The hot water in which he soaked his boxers became like an infused humidifier which now permeated throughout the whole apartment. The smell was almost overpowering. Half asleep, he threw the water down the drain, and then got ready for work. This whole tobacco thing would not have been an issue, except for the fact that he had promised his wife that he would quit smoking. While the shisha was usually excluded from this ban, his wife had insisted, and to avoid additional conflict, he had given in once again and he had lied to her.

He was happy to have shipped her and the kids back to Amman for the summer months as usual; and it made his life easier that that had pleased her, too. Returning to an empty flat for weeks on end was heaven. He could revert to his pre-marital careless inconsiderate laziness – at least within the confines of his outrageously expensive, ill-maintained, two-bedroom penthouse.

Somewhere between the boiling hot weather, the scorching rent, the nagging of his mother and his wife, he resigned himself to the fact that his world will never be what he expected. Still, he loved Dubai. This was a city he could truly identify with. It understood him and allowed him to invent and reinvent himself as they both got older, bolder and more experienced – and as the audience grew and continued to change. It was a relatively easy thing to do. A simple marketing campaign was enough, no one would bother to delve deeper. Over the years since his arrival in 1985, he had slowly and meticulously painted the dry landscape of his dull existence green; he said that he had studied at Stanford and graduated with honours; that he had rejected an exceptional job offer in the US so that he could come back and work in an Arab country; that he had never applied for a green card because he was simply too busy and it was not that important to him; that his elder brother who was a clerk at the Ministry of Defense was a general in the national army; and his father who was a humble, unambitious bank manager was one of the pillars of Amman. This fable, however, did not protect him from being overlooked when it came to promotions as the barely 30-something, inexperienced, recently hired auditor from the UK received a promotion far exceeding his own salary after 15 years of dedication to the same company. He has often wondered if he could have done more to get more out of life. But what is doing more, he would ask himself? And everything always ended up being a big waste of time.

He had once believed that if you have the right ingredients, you can create magic anywhere, that's the magic of magic.

Saturday 8th September

Tan left hand with wedding ring on.
Get rid of honeyed tobacco scent.

When he woke up this morning, the scent of the honeyed tobacco had enveloped him. That particular corner where he had flung his boxers the night before emitted a strong scent which had embedded itself into the very fibres of the carpet and was slowly inching its way across the apartment. He now had to shampoo the carpet as well.

He started using every opportunity to make sure his left hand was exposed to plenty of hot, burning sun. He drove to his office that morning with his hand dangling out of the window holding a cigarette he never smoked but which was a necessary excuse to open his car window in this heat; and when he drove from his office to the mall, he did the same.

Going to the mall on a daily basis started off as a way to avoid the traffic. Rather than spending close to an hour getting home, he came up with the ingenious idea of stopping off at the nearest mall – and there were plenty to choose from. He personally preferred Mall of the Emirates. He would have a cup of coffee at Starbucks – which he kept promising himself he would boycott – he would read the papers and move on an hour or so later. His plan was so ingenious that everyone else had also thought of it. As a result the mall and coffee-shops were usually packed, and Sheikh Zayed Road was almost as congested two hours later. But this did not deter him from his plan, for he discovered, like every other hot-blooded man, that this was a perfectly respectable place to openly ogle the multicultural, fashion-victimised female population.

When he got home again that night, he could not escape Khan's eyes. The watchman had a special liking for his wife who always gave him little gifts and, some evenings, leftovers from their hot meals, but did not care much for him. This was mainly because he had caught him once peeping in on his wife from the roof. They lived in a penthouse apartment with a rooftop 'garden', and Khan had the key to the upper roof where all the air-conditioners, water tanks and TV satellites stood. One evening he arrived home to find Khan peeping through the skylight. It's true that his wife was not at all exposed, and he never told her about the incident, but he made it very clear to Khan that he would hold it like a sword over his neck. He tried, unsuccessfully, not to give too much thought to the threatening message Khan's eyes conveyed.

When he reached his apartment, he doused his boxers with laundry powder and left them to soak overnight in hot boiling water.

Friday 7th September

Just one job today: find wedding ring and tan left hand with it on.

The aroma of honeyed tobacco clung to him, and so did the

beautiful Titiana. He knew very well what attracted him to her, but he could not figure out what on earth drew her to him. He had only one week to readjust to the fact of his being a husband and father. To reinstate himself and his surroundings to what his wife considered appropriate. To clear out all evidence of ever having enjoyed his few revitalizing moments as a bachelor. To rinse away any stubborn inspirational stains from his soul. What was he supposed to do with Titiana seven days and counting from his wife's arrival? That was what he kept asking himself, as he watched her cross her legs and slip a slender foot out of her shoes. He was simultaneously thinking of coloured and flavoured condoms, when the memory of where he had left his wedding band popped into his head.

Today was his last day of absolute freedom... until next summer. He vaguely recalled seeing Khan's surprised face as he drove Titiana home, which turned out to be close to his own, opposite Al Karama. He went home to an empty bed, dragging frayed dreams which he hoped would be prolonged by having an amazing creature like Titiana in the confined proximity of his car.

He flung his boxers into the corner of his bedroom just before he closed his eyes and fell asleep.

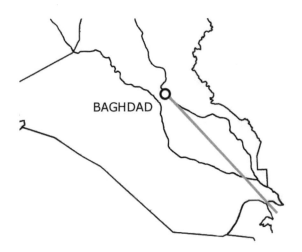

The Reality and the Record

Hassan Blasim

Everyone staying at the refugee reception centre has two stories – the real one and the one for the record. The stories for the record are the ones the new refugees tell to obtain the right to humanitarian asylum, written down in the immigration department and preserved in their private files. The real stories remain locked in the hearts of the refugees, for them to mull over in complete secrecy. That's not to say it's easy to tell the two stories apart. They merge and it becomes impossible to distinguish them. Two days ago a new Iraqi refugee arrived in Malmo in southern Sweden. They took him to the reception centre and did some medical tests on him. Then they gave him a room, a bed, a towel, a bedsheet, a bar of soap, a knife, fork and spoon, and a cooking pot. Today the man is sitting in front of the immigration officer telling his story at amazing speed, while the immigration officer asks him to slow down as much as possible.

They told me they had sold me to another group and they were very cheerful. They stayed up all night drinking whisky and laughing. They even invited me to join them in a drink but I declined and told them I was a religious man. They bought me new clothes, and that night they cooked me a chicken and served me fruit and sweets. It seems I fetched a good price. The leader of the group even shed real tears when he said goodbye. He embraced me like a brother. 'You're a very good man. I wish you all the best, and good luck in your life,' said the man with one eye.

I think I stayed with the first group just three months. They had kidnapped me on that cold accursed night. That was in the early winter of 2006. We had orders to go to the Tigris and it was the first time we had received instructions directly from the head of the Emergency Department in the hospital. At the bank of the river the policemen were standing around six headless bodies. The heads had been put in an empty flour sack in front of the bodies. The police guessed they were the bodies of some clerics. We had arrived late because of the heavy rain. The police piled the bodies onto the ambulance driven by my colleague Abu Salim and I carried the sack of heads to my ambulance. The streets were empty and the only sounds to break the forlorn silence of the Baghdad night were some gunshots in the distance and the noise of an American helicopter patrolling over the Green Zone. We set off along Abu Nawas Street towards Rashid Street, driving at medium speed because of the rain. I remembered the words the director of the emergency department in the hospital often used to say: 'When you're carrying an injured person or a patient close to death, the speed of the ambulance shows how humane and responsible you are.' But when you are carrying severed heads in an ambulance, you needn't go faster than a hearse drawn by mules in a dark mediaeval forest. The director saw himself as a philosopher and an artist, but 'born in the wrong country' as he would say. He took his work seriously nonetheless and considered it a sacred duty, because to him running the ambulance section of the emergency department meant managing the dividing line between life and death. We called him the Professor and my other colleagues hated him and called him mad. I know why they hated him, because the enigmatic and aggressive way he spoke made him seem screwed up in the eyes of others. But I retained much respect and affection for him because of the beautiful and fascinating things he said. Once he said to me: 'Spilt blood and superstition are the basis of the world. Man is not the only creature who kills for bread, or love, or power, because animals in the jungle do that in various ways, but he is the only creature who kills because of faith.' He would usually wrap up his speeches by pointing to the sky and declaiming theatrically: 'The question of humanity can be solved only by constant dread.' My colleague Abu Salim had a notion that the Professor had links with the terrorist groups because of the violent language he used, but I would loyally defend the man, because they did not understand that he was a philosopher who refused to make foolish jokes, as the stupid ambulance drivers did all day. I remembered every sentence and every word he said, for I was captivated by my affection and admiration for him.

Let me get back to that wretched night. When we turned towards the Martyrs Bridge I noticed that the ambulance driven by Abu Salim had disappeared. Then in the side mirror I caught sight of a police car catching up with us at high speed. I pulled over to the side in the middle of the bridge. Four young men in masks and special police uniforms got out of the police car. The leader of the group pointed his pistol in my face and told me to get out of the vehicle, while his colleagues unloaded the sack of heads from the ambulance.

'I've been kidnapped and they are going to cut off my head.' That was my first thought when they tied me up and stuffed me in the trunk of the police car. It took me only 10 minutes to realize what was awaiting me. I recited the Throne Verse from the Quran three times in the darkness of the trunk and I felt that my skin was starting to peel off. For some reason in those dark moments I thought about my body weight, maybe 70 kilos. The slower the car went, or the more it turned, the more frightened I was, and when it picked up speed again a strange blend of tranquility and anxiety would pulse through me. Perhaps I thought at those moments of what the Professor had said about the correlation between the speed and the imminence of death. I didn't understand exactly what he meant, but he would say that someone about to die in the forest would be more afraid than someone about to die in a speeding ambulance, because the first one feels that fate has singled him out, while the second imagines there are others sticking with him. I also remember that he once announced with a smile: 'I would like to have my death in a spaceship travelling at the speed of light.'

I imagined that all the unidentified and mutilated bodies I had carried in the ambulance since the fall of Baghdad lay before me, and that in the darkness surrounding me I then saw the Professor picking my severed head from a pile of rubbish, while my colleagues made dirty jokes about my liking for the Professor. I don't think the police car drove very far before it came to a halt. At least they did not leave the city. I tried to remember the Rahman Verse of the Quran but they got me out of the car and escorted me into a house which smelt of grilled fish. I could hear a child crying. They undid my blindfold and I found myself in a cold, unfurnished room. Then three madmen laid into me and beat me to a pulp, until a darkness again descended.

I thought I heard a cock crow at first. I shut my eyes but I couldn't sleep. I felt a sharp pain in my left ear. With difficulty I turned over onto my back and pushed myself towards the window, which had recently been blocked up. I was very thirsty. It was easy to work out that I was in a house in one of Baghdad's old neighbourhoods. In fact I don't know exactly what details of my story matter to you, for me to get the right of asylum in your country. I find it very hard to describe those days of terror, but I want to mention also some of the things which matter to me. I felt that God, and behind him the Professor, would never abandon me throughout my ordeal. I felt the presence of God intensely in my heart, nurturing my peace of mind and calling me to patience. The Professor kept my mind busy and alleviated the loneliness of my captivity. He was my solace and my comfort. Throughout those arduous months I would recall what the Professor had said about his friend, Dawoud the engineer. What did he mean by saying that the world is all interconnected? And where do the power and the will of God stand in such matters? We were drinking tea at the hospital door when the Professor said: 'While my friend Dawoud was driving the family car through the streets of Baghdad, an Iraqi poet in London was writing a fiery article in praise of the resistance, with a bottle of whisky on the table in front of him to help harden his heart. Because the world is all interconnected, through feelings, words, nightmares, and other secret channels. Out of the poet's article jumped three masked men. They stopped the family car and killed Dawoud, his wife, his child and his father. His mother was waiting for them at home. Dawoud's mother doesn't know the Iraqi poet nor the masked men. She knows how to cook the fish which was awaiting them. The Iraqi poet fell asleep on the sofa in London in a drunken stupor, while Dawoud's mother's fish went cold and the sun set in Baghdad.'

The wooden door of the room opened and a young man, tall with a pale and haggard face, came in carrying breakfast. He smiled at me as he put the food down in front of me. At first I was uncertain what I could say or do. But then I threw myself at his feet and implored him tearfully: 'I am the father of three children… I'm a religious man who fears God… I have nothing to do with politics or religious denominations… God protect you… I'm just an ambulance driver… before the invasion, and since the invasion… I swear by God and his noble Prophet.' The young man put a finger to his lips and rushed out. I felt that my end had come. I drank the cup of tea and performed my prayers in the hope that God would forgive my sins. At the second prostration I felt that a layer of ice was forming across my body and I almost cried out in fear, but the young man opened the door, carrying a small lighting device attached to a stand, and accompanied by a boy carrying a Kalashnikov rifle. The boy stood next to me, pointing the gun at my head, and from then on he did not leave his place. A fat man in his forties came in, taking no notice of me. On the wall he hung a black cloth banner inscribed with a Quranic verse urging Muslims to fight jihad. Then a masked man came in with a video camera and a small computer. Then a boy came in with a small wooden table. The masked man joked with the boy, tweaked his nose and thanked him, then put the computer on the table and busied himself with setting up the camera in front of the black banner. The thin young man tried out the lighting system three times and then left.

'Abu Jihad, Abu Jihad,' the fat man shouted.

The young man's voice came from outside the room: 'Wait a minute. Right you are, Abu Arkan.'

This time the young man came back carrying the sack of heads which they had taken from the ambulance. Everyone blocked their nose because of the stink from the sack. The fat man asked me to sit in front of the black banner. I felt that my legs were paralysed, but the fat man pulled me roughly by my shirt collar. At that point another man came in, thick-set with one eye, and ordered the fat man to let me be. This man had in his hand an army uniform. The man with one eye sat close to me, with his arm across my shoulders like a friend, and asked me to calm down. He told me they wouldn't slaughter me if I was cooperative and kind-hearted. I didn't understand fully what he meant by this 'kind-hearted'. He told me it would only take a few minutes. The one-eyed man took a small piece of paper from his pocket and asked me to read it. Meanwhile the fat man was taking the decomposing heads out of the sack and lining them up in front of me. It said on the piece of paper that I was an officer in the Iraqi army and these were the heads of other officers, and that accompanied by my fellow officers I had raided houses, raped women and tortured innocent civilians, that we had received orders to kill from a senior officer in the U.S. Army, in return for large financial rewards. The man with one eye asked me to put on the army uniform and the cameraman asked everyone to pull back behind the camera. Then he came up to me and started adjusting my head, as a hairdresser does. After that he adjusted the line of heads, then went back behind the camera and called out: 'Off you go.'

The cameraman's voice was very familiar. Perhaps it resembled the voice of a famous actor, or it might have been like the voice of the Professor when he was making an exaggerated effort to talk softly. After they filmed the videotape, I didn't meet the members of the group again, other than the young man who brought me food, and he prevented me from asking any questions. Every time he brought food he would tell me a new joke about politicians and men of religion. My only wish was that he would let me contact my wife, because I had hidden some money for a rainy day in a place where even the jinn would never think of looking, but they vehemently rejected my request. The one-eyed leader of the group told me that everything depended on the success of the videotape, and in fact the tape was such a success so quickly that everyone was surprised. Al Jazeera broadcast the videotape. They allowed me to watch television and on that day they were jumping for joy, so much so that the fat man kissed me on the head and said I was a great actor. What made me angry was the Al Jazeera newsreader, who assured viewers that the channel had established through reliable sources that the tape was authentic and that the Ministry of Defence had admitted that the officers had gone missing. After the success of the broadcast they started treating me in a manner which was better than good. They took trouble over my food and bedding and allowed me to have a bath. Their kindness culminated on the night they sold me to the second group. Then three masked men from that group came into the room and, after the man with one eye had given me a warm farewell, the new men laid into me with their fists, tied me up and gagged me, then shoved me into the boot of a car which drove off at terrifying speed.

The second group's car travelled far this time. Perhaps we reached the outskirts of Baghdad. They took me out in a desolate village where dogs roamed and barked all over the place. They held me in a cow pen and there were two men who took turns guarding the pen night and day. I don't know why, but they proceeded to starve me and humiliate me. They were completely different from the first group. They wore their masks all the time and never spoke a word with me. They would communicate with each other through gestures. In fact there was not a human voice to be heard from the village, just the barking of dogs the whole month I spent in the cow pen. The hours passed with oppressive tedium. I would hope that anything would happen, rather than this life sentence with three cows. I gave up thinking about these people, or what religious group or party they belonged to. I no longer bemoaned my fate but felt I had already lived through what happened to me at some time, and that time was a period that would not last long. But my sense of this time made it seem slow and confused. It no longer occurred to me to try to escape or to ask them what they wanted from me. I felt that I was carrying out some mission, a binding duty which I had to perform until my last breath. Perhaps there was a secret power working in league with a human power to play a secret game for purposes too grand for a simple man like me to grasp. 'Every man has both a poetic obligation and a human obligation,' as the Professor used to say. But if that was true, how could I tell the difference, and easily, between the limits of the human obligation and those of the poetic obligation? Because my understanding is that, for example, looking after my wife and children is one of my human obligations, and refusing to hate is a poetic obligation. But why did the Professor say that we confuse the two obligations and do not recognize the diabolical element that drives them both? Because the diabolic obligations imply the capacity to stand in the face of a man when he is pushing his own humanity towards the abyss, and this is too much for the mind of a simple man like me, who barely completed his intermediate education, at least I think so.

What I'm saying has nothing to do with my asylum

request. What matters to you is the horror. If the Professor was here, he would say that the horror lies in the simplest of puzzles which shine in a cold star in the sky over this city. In the end they came into the cow pen after midnight one night. One of the masked men spread one corner of the pen with fine carpets. Then his companion hung a black banner inscribed: The Islamic Jihad Group, Iraq Branch. Then the cameraman came in with his camera, and it struck me that he was the same cameraman as the one with the first group. His hand gestures were the same as those of the first cameraman. The only difference was that he was now communicating with the others with gestures. They asked me to put on a white dishdasha and sit in front of the black banner. They gave me a piece of paper and told me to read out what was written on it: that I belonged to the Mehdi Army and I was a famous killer, I had cut off the heads of hundreds of Sunni men, and I had support from Iran. Before I'd finished reading, one of the cows gave a loud moo, so the cameraman asked me to read it again. One of the men took the three cows away so that we could finish off the cow pen scene.

I later realised that everyone who bought me was moving me across the same bridge. I don't know why. One group would take me across the Martyrs Bridge towards Karkh on the west bank of the Tigris, then the next group would take me back across the same bridge to Rasafa on the east bank. If I go on like this, I think my story will never end, and I'm worried you'll say what others have said about my story. So I think it would be best if I summarise the story for you, rather than have you accuse me of making it up. They sold me to a third group. The car drove at speed across the Martyrs Bridge once again. I was moved to a luxurious house and this time my prison was a bedroom with a lovely comfortable bed, the kind in which you see film stars having sex. My fear evaporated and I began to grasp the concept of the secret mission for which they had chosen me. I carried out the mission so as not to lose my head, but I also thought I would test their reaction in certain matters. After filming a new video in which I spoke about how I belonged to Sunni Islamist groups and about my work blowing up Shi'ite mosques and public markets, I asked them for some money as payment for making the tape. Their decisive response was a beating I will never forget. Throughout the year and a half of my kidnapping experience, I was moved from one hiding place to another. They shot video of me talking about how I was a treacherous Kurd, an infidel Christian, a Saudi terrorist, a Syrian Baathist intelligence agent, or a Revolutionary Guard from Zoroastrian Iran. On these videotapes I murdered, raped, started fires, planted bombs and carried out crimes that no sane person would even imagine. All these tapes were broadcast on satellite channels around the world. Experts, journalists and politicians sat there discussing what I said and did. The only bad luck we ran into was when we made a video in which I appeared as a Spanish soldier, with a resistance fighter holding a knife to my neck, demanding Spanish forces withdraw from Iraq. All the satellite stations refused to broadcast the tape because Spanish forces had left the country a year earlier. I almost paid a heavy price for this mistake when the group holding me wanted to kill me in revenge for what had happened, but the cameraman saved me by suggesting another wonderful idea, the last of my videotape roles. They dressed me in the costume of an Afghan fighter, trimmed my beard and put a black turban on my head. Five men stood behind me and they brought in six men screaming and crying out for help from God, his Prophet and the Prophet's family. They slaughtered the men in front of me like sheep as I announced that I was the new leader of the al Qaida organization in Mesopotamia and made threats against everyone in creation.

Late one night the cameraman brought me my old clothes and took me to the ambulance, which was standing at the door. They put those six heads in a sack and threw it into the vehicle. At that moment I noticed the cameraman's gestures and I thought that surely he was the cameraman for all the groups and maybe the mastermind of this dreadful game. I sat behind the steering wheel with trembling hands. Then the cameraman gave the order from behind his mask: 'You know the way. Cross the Martyrs Bridge, to the hospital.'

I am asking for asylum in your country because of everyone. They are all killers and schemers – my wife, my children, my neighbours, my colleagues, God, his Prophet, the government, the newspapers, even the Professor whom I thought an angel, and now I have suspicions that the cameraman with the terrorist groups was the Professor himself. His enigmatic language was merely proof of his connivance and his vile nature. They all told me I hadn't been away for a year and half, because I came back the morning after working that rainy night, and on that very morning the Professor said to me: 'The world is just a bloody and hypothetical story, and we are all killers and heroes.' And those six heads cannot be proof of what I'm saying, just as they are not proof that the night will not spread across the sky.

Three days after this story was filed away in the records of the immigration department, they took the man who told it to the psychiatric hospital. Before the doctor could start asking him about his childhood memories, the ambulance driver summed up his real story in four words: 'I want to sleep.'

It was a humble entreaty.

Translated from the Arabic by Jonathan Wright

Authors

Hassan Blasim was born in Baghdad in 1973. He is a poet, writer and filmmaker and co-editor of www.iraqstory.com. He currently lives in Finland.

Elias Farkouh was born in Amman in 1948. A novelist and short story writer, he has published seven short story collections – including *Ihda wa Eshrouna Talqa lil-Nabeyy* ('Twenty One Shots for the Prophet'), which won the 1982 Jordanian Writers Association Award, *Tuyour Amman Tuhalliq Munkhafida* ('Amman's Birds Sweep Low', 1981), *Al-Saf'a* ('The Slap', 1997), and *Huqoul Al-Zilal* ('Fields of Shadows', 2002) – and three novels. His first novel, *Kamaat Uz-Zabad,* translated as *Foam Statures*, won the State Encouragement Award in 1990. His third novel 'The Land of Purgatory' was shortlisted for the inaugural International Prize for Arabic Fiction and won the Jordanian Writers' Association Award of the novel in 2008. Elias has also won the State Meritorious Award (1997) and the Mahmud Sayf Ed-Din Irani Award (awarded by the Jordanian Writers' Association), both for his short story writing. His work in literary translation, *Other Fires*, a volume of short stories by women writers from Latin America, appeared in 1999. In 1991 he founded Dar Azminah, his own publishing house.

Gamal al-Ghitani, is the founding editor of the weekly newspaper *Akhbar Al-Adab* – for many, the Arab world's most

165

active literary-cultural resource. He began his career as a war reporter and a left-wing activist, before embarking on a career in cultural journalism. Born in Juhaina, Sohag, Al-Ghitani grew up in Cairo, and became one of the founders of the literary magazine *Gallery 68,* as well as a central figure in the city's café culture, and for many years the friend and confidante of the late Nobel laureate Naguib Mahfouz. His writing works to reconnect the stylistics of the Arab literary cannon with the grassroots vernacular of urban discourse. His best known novel in English is *Zaini Barakat* (Penguin) which mimics the cadences and rhythms of canonical Arabic to retell the story of the Ottoman takeover of Egypt. He received the Lora Betlouine Award for translated literature, the highest French award to be bestowed upon non-French writers, for his book *Al-Tagalyat Illuminations* (2205). In 2007 he was awarded Egypt's State Merit Award.

Nedim Gürsel has been described by Yashar Kemal as 'one of the few contemporary Turkish writers who have brought something new to our literature.' Born in Gaziantep, Turkey, in 1951, Gürsel was forced – after the coup d'état in 1971 – to testify in court over one of his articles, which lead to his temporarily exile in France, where he studied at the Sorbonne. Gürsel then returned to Turkey, but the military putsch of 1980 sent him back into exile in France. He was awarded the Prize of the Academy of Turkish Linguistics and Literature for his first major prose work, *A Long Summer in Istanbul* (1975), which has been translated into several languages. In 1986, his novel *La Première Femme* received the Ipeçki Prize for its contribution to conciliation between the Greek and Turkish peoples. His autobiography *Au Pays des Poissons Captifs* was recently published simultaneously in France and Turkey. His first novel to be translated into English, *The Conqueror*, is about to be published by Talisman, New York.

AUTHORS

Joumana Haddad (1970, Beirut) is a poet, translator and journalist. She is head of the cultural pages in prestigious *An Nahar* newspaper, as well as the administrator of the IPAF Literary Prize (often referred to as the 'Arab Booker') and the editor-in-chief of *Jasad* magazine, an Arabic cultural magazine specialising in the literature and arts of the body. She has published several widely acclaimed poetry collections, including *I Did Not Commit Enough Errors, Lilith's Return, The Panther Hiding at the Base of her Shoulders, Bad Habits,* and *The Mirrors of Passers By.* Her books have been translated into many languages and published internationally. Speaking seven languages, she has also published several works of translation, including a compilation of Lebanese modern poetry in Spanish, and more recently an anthology of 150 poets who committed suicide in the 20th century.

Ala Hlehel was born in Jesh, Galilee, in 1974 and graduated from the Tel Aviv School of Screenwriting and Haifa University. He has written numerous short stories, plays, and scripts for film and TV, and in 2003 he took part in an international playwrights' residency at the Royal Court, London. He has received a number of awards for his work, among them the 2003 Young Writer Award from the AM Qattan Foundation. Ala has also worked as a radio presenter in Haifa and has published three books to date: *The Circus* (a novel); *Stories for the Time of Need* (short stories) and *The Father, the Son and the Lost Spirit* (novel & five short stories). He lives in Akka.

Yitzhak Laor is a poet, author and journalist. He was born in Pardes Hanna, and completed his degree in Theatre and Literature at Tel Aviv University. He is the author of five poetry books, most recently *Leviathan City*, 19 novels, most recently *Ecce Homo*, plays, and article collections. He is best known for his poetry of political protest, particularly about the Lebanese War of 1982 and the Israeli occupation of Palestine.

Laor writes literary criticism for the *Ha`aretz* newspaper, is a founder and editor of the literary journal *Mita'am* and works and writes in Tel Aviv. He was recently awarded the Amichai Poetry Prize (2007).

Yousef al-Mohaimeed was born in Riyadh, Saudi Arabia, in 1964 and has published several novels and short-story collections in Arabic. His novels include *Al-Qaroura* ('The Bottle'), *The Dolphin's Excursion, and Wolves of the Crescent Moon*. The latter was published in English by Penguin USA and in French by Actes Sud (both 2007). All of his novels are widely published in the Arab world but banned in his own country.

Fadwa al-Qasem is a Palestinian author, born in Libya (1963), with Canadian citizenship. Her short stories have appeared in *Akhbar Al Adab* (Cairo), *Al Adab Magazine* and *Al Hayat* Newspaper (Lebanon), and *Al Bayan* (UAE), and in English in *Banipal #27, In Our Own Words* (USA), as well as on websites. She keeps a bilingual blog – www.gypsyexpress. com – and works as the Creative Director of Tabeer, a company providing bilingual content and translation services. Her first collection of short stories in Arabic *The Scent of Cardamom*, was published by Dar Sharqiyat in 2005. She is currently working on translating this collection into English and on her second collection of Arabic short stories.

Nabil Sulayman was born in 1945 and graduated from Damascus University in 1967. He founded Al-Hiwar publishing house in 1970, the same year that he published his first novel, now one of 16, along with 24 books of literary criticism and other cultural themes. He has lectured in many a number of Arab countries, as well as in Madrid and Austin, Texas.

Translators

Aron Aji is a dean at St. Ambrose University, Davenport, Iowa, USA. A native of Turkey, he has translated fiction, poetry and plays by Turkish writers into English. His translation of Bilge Karasu's *The Garden of Departed Cats* (New Directions) won the 2004 National Translation Award. Aji also received a 2006 National Endowment for the Arts fellowship for his current translation project, another novel by Karasu, *The Evening of a Very Long Day*.

Anthony Calderbank has lived in the Arab World for many years. He has translated a number of novels and short stories from Arabic into English including works by Egyptian and Saudi writers, including Wolves of the Crescent Moon by Yousef Al-Mohaimeed, Rhadopis of Nubia by Naguib Mahfouz, and The Tent by Miral Al-Tahawy. He is currently based in Riyadh.

Alice Guthrie is a freelance translator of Arabic, Spanish and French, and an activist on Palestinian issues, international migration and freedom of movement. She is currently working on a translation of Rachid Nini's account of his time as an 'illegal' in Spain and France, *Diaries of a Clandestine Migrant*. She studied written Arabic at Exeter University and at IFEAD, Damascus, and dialectical Arabic in Syria, Lebanon, and Algeria.

R. Neil Hewison a graduate of York University, has lived and worked in Egypt since 1979. He is the translator of *City of Love and Ashes* by Yusuf Idris and *Wedding Night* by Yusuf Abu Rayya (winner of the Naguib Mahfouz Medal for Literature), and the author of *The Fayoum: History and Guide.*

William Maynard Hutchins is an American who has taught in Ghana, Lebanon, Egypt, and France, in addition to the United States. He has translated *Cairo Modern* and *The Cairo Trilogy* by Naguib Mahfouz and Anubis and *The Seven Veils of Seth* by Ibrahim al-Koni, among other novels.

Nancy Rogers, a native of Wichita, Kansas, has translated works in the areas of modern Arabic literature, current events, Islamic law, Islamic thought and history, and Muslim-Christian relations. She lives with her husband and two daughters in Amman, Jordan.

Jonathan Wright studied Arabic at Oxford University in the 1970s and has spent 18 of the past 30 years in the Arab world, mostly as a journalist with the international news agency Reuters. His first major literary translation was of Khaled el-Khamissi's best-selling book *Taxi*, published in English by Aflame Books in 2008.

Special Thanks

The editor and publisher would like to thank the following people for their advice and support throughout the project: Tuncay Birkan, Mona Baker, Ilan Pappé, Rachel Stevens, Kim Haskins, Ali Sheikholeslami, Christin Stein, Rachel Feldberg, Tania Hershman, Mirjana Cibulka, Ross Bradshaw, Tony Rudolph, David Eckersall, Michael Paulin, Tom Spooner, Isaac Shaffer, Cathy Bolton, Kate Griffin, Avril Heffernan, Will Carr, Maria Ruben and Akl Awit.

ALSO AVAILABLE IN THE SERIES...

Decapolis
Tales from Ten Cities

Ed. Maria Crossan

ISBN 9781905583034
RRP: £7.95

Featuring:
Larissa Boehning (Berlin), David Constantine (Manchester), Arnon Grunberg (Amsterdam), Emil Hakl (Prague), Amanda Michalopoulou (Athens), Empar Moliner (Barcelona), Aldo Nove (Milan), Jacques Réda (Paris), Dalibor Šimpraga (Zagreb), Ágúst Borgþór Sverrisson (Reykjavik).

Decapolis is a book which imagines the city otherwise. Bringing together ten writers from across Europe, it offers snapshots of their native cities, freezing for a moment the characters and complexities that define them. Ten cities: diverse, incompatible, contradictory – in everything from language to landscape.

'Europe is heavy with history and the trace left by cataclysm and upheaval. These are present in these tales, and yet coexist with a kind of wry and knowing playfulness.'
– A.S. Byatt in *The Times*

'The European short story is clearly in vigorous form.'
– Matthew Sweet, *Nightwaves, Radio 3*

'A fine, streetwise cacophony'
– *The Independent*

Elsewhere
Stories from Small Town Europe

ED. MARIA CROSSAN

ISBN: 978 1905583133
RRP: £7.95.

Featuring:
Gyrdir Eliasson (Iceland), Frode Grytten (Norway), Micheal O Conghaile (Ireland), Danielle Picard (France), Mehmet Zaman Saclioglu (Turkey), Ingo Schulze (Germany), Roman Simic (Croatia), Jean Sprackland (England), Olga Tokarczuk (Poland), Mirja Unge (Sweden)

What do we mean by 'small town'? How has this innocuous term - one up from 'village', a couple down from 'city' - come to function as a pejorative? Pressed to describe what the phrase 'small town' conjures up, we'd be hard pushed to say anything positive: closed-minded; petty; provincial; parochial. On a broad European canvas, however, the rich traditions of short story writing challenge these preconceptions. The stories collected here are neither narrow-minded nor petty, nor do the minds of their protagonists contract to fit their environment.

In Germany, a house-husband is slowly sent over the edge by his over-achieving neighbours. In the town of Odda in Norway, a middle-aged Morrissey fan has a matter of hours to find a girlfriend so his ailing mother can die in peace. It's the small gestures - a white lie, the turning of a blind eye, a small kindness or a secret kept - that allow the characters of these communities to survive, to breathe easily within the seemingly tight strictures life there can impose. It's how we do things round here...